BEING
ABBAS
EL ABD

AHMED ALAIDY

Translated by

HUMPHREY DAVIES

Arabia Books
London

First published in Great Britain in 2008 by
Arabia Books
26 Cadogan Court
Draycott Avenue
London SW3 3BX
www.hauspublishing.co.uk

This edition published by arrangement with
The American University in Cairo Press
113 Sharia Kasr el Aini, Cairo, Egypt
420 Fifth Avenue, New York, NY 10018
www.aucpress.com

First published in Arabic in 2003 as *An takun 'Abbas al-'Abd*
Copyright © 2003 by Ahmed Alaidy
The moral right of the author has been asserted
Protected by the Berne Convention

English translation copyright © 2006 by Humphrey Davies

ISBN 978-1-906697-05-1
Printed in Egypt
1 2 3 4 5 6 7 8 9 10   14 13 12 11 10 09 08

Cover design: Arabia Books
Design: AUC Press

For Hadly

To my partners in crime, in order of involvement:
my father and mother;
my mentors Chuck Palahniuk, Mohamed Hashem, Sonallah
Ibrahim, Ibrahim Mansour, Badr el Rifa'i, Ibrahim Dawoud,
Hamdi Abu Glayyil, Ahmad Khaled Tawfiq, and Bilal Fadl;
my friends Muhammad Alaa el Din and Muhammad Fathi;
and the ceiling of my room, which contained me when the
world moved a few centimeters forward.

Sworn under oath,
Ahmed Alaidy

An Introduction You Can Suck or Shove

SHE WASN'T A CORPSE YET.

Hind doesn't like wasting time because she's never been like other girls.

Place: Geneina Mall, the Ladies' Toilet.

Hind writes the mobile phone number on the insides of the doors of the toilets with a waterproof lipstick, then passes a Kleenex soaked in soda water over it, 'cos that way, cupcake, it can't be wiped off!

I told her to write it at the eye level of a person sitting on the toilet seat.

Above it two words: **CALL ME**

Why?

Because these things happen.

The woman goes into the toilet to relieve herself.

The woman goes into the toilet to use something that emerges, from her handbag, to protect her.

Her sin, of which she is guiltless.

A naked fragile butterfly—and

Enter the terrible number.

The number gazes at her weakness.

The number *permits itself* to intervene instantaneously.

The number asks no permission and has no supernumeraries.

The number is

Zero-one-zero, six, forty, ninety, thirty.

CALL ME
010 6 40 90 30

Arkadia Mall:
CALL ME
010 6 40 90 30

Ramses Hilton Mall:
CALL ME
010 6 40 90 30

The World Trade Center:

Accept no imitations.

Zero-one-zero, six, forty, ninety, thirty.

CALL ME

There's a thing I like to get up to from time to time.

As though I was living like any other lunatic.

As though I was myself, with all the little stupidities I like to
commit.

And with all the stupidities that have become—by now—part
of my make-up, it was obvious I'd ask her to push it.

How far?

You guess.

Chapter 1

THERE ARE THINGS AND THERE ARE THINGS.

There are things that ruin your day just by being there,

and there are things you'd prefer to keep at a distance . . .

over there. . . .

Over theeeeeeeeeeeeeeeeeeeeeeeeeeeeeeeeeeeeeeeeeeere!

Who am I?

I am I and I have my reasons and I have no reason to be indebted to you or anyone else. My only ambition is to survive on my own, in one piece, and for the whole world, as a ball of wax, to go to hell.

I am the one in whose face others have so often spat that that sweet dirty feeling has grown and built up in my constricted chest. . . .

There are things and there are things. . . .

Now, tell me . . .

Have you ever tried running a red light in front of a bunch of traffic cops sagging with gold braid without being a "Don't-you-know-who-I-am?" or head of some state or other?

Have you ever tried taking a cigarette from a pack in your sleeping father's pocket?

Do you spit in every cup of tea they bring you so no one else will drink from it?

Have you ever tasted the blood draining out of you during a dialogue of fists with someone older and bigger?

Have you ever wanted to slam a plate of hot soup into the face of your relative who doesn't know your name but tells you how 'sweet' a cup of tea from your very own hands would be?

Have you ever tried sticking out your tongue at a giant saw? No?!

Look at me. I'm on my knees to you now. Give your exasperated patience its head.

NOW.

SCREAM

in the faces of the traffic cops

in the face of your father

in the faces of café acquaintances just passing through

and of your relatives whom you don't know—

*Stop **JUDGING ME!***

ACCEPT ME AS I AM NOT AS YOU WANT ME TO BE!

There are things and there are things . . .

Your pitiful face announces that you will fall prey to things you do not know. I know you don't give a genteel shit about that but please, don't be afraid:

I have done worse.

Come close, little one.

Commmmmmmme.

Approach without real guarantees or promises of any sort.

I will never protect you or love you or be at your side if you need me, and you will find out why you should feel grateful for that.

You will learn how to feel pain when I jump over the barbed
wire fences that surround everything you fear and hate,
Because I won't be jumping out, I'll be jumping in, to where
there are a thousand things that make you say:
"I can't stand this any more, I can't bear that any more, not
any more, not any more, not any more, not any more."
What is madness?
It doesn't matter.
Who am I really?
. . .
Now you can be afraid
For together we shall taste insanity
Sip by sip.

Chapter 2

Don't believe her.
She will tell you of crimes I never committed and will weep in your arms in the hope that your heart will soften or relent.
She will give you of herself things that will alter your being, and you know very well how much a woman who is good at giving can take.
This is the truth in all its cruelty, so do as you damn well please.

I WAKE UP, LATE AS USUAL, TO THE FOUL-MOUTHED YELLING OF THE neighbors.
Today's lesson is a painful one and goes:
Nothing can teach you better how to bawl someone out than a wife who's hot for it and loses all sense of proportion on catching sight of a bed.
I call Abbas on the phone in the apartment of his elderly neighbor, a lady afflicted with Alzheimer's, and then I explain to her—as usual—who I am and who he is and ask her, with

a show of good manners: "Could you possibly call him over?"

"Certainly, sonny, certainly."

The old lady puts down the receiver and comes back after a reasonable length of time and says that he'll talk to me "when he's finished something he has in hand."

She asks me how I am.

"Same old stuff,"

and "Not too bad,"

and "Thanks for asking."

The usual clichés you say if you can't find anything else to vomit down the receiver.

I read the morning paper in the bathroom, have breakfast, drink my tea. I crack my knuckles in front of the television and when the morning movie finishes I try him again.

Abbas won't answer, but I pick up the receiver anyway.

"Hallo."

I know Abbas won't answer, and so does Abbas.

"Yes. Who is it?"

"Abbas's friend from work, ma'am."

"Abbas who??"

God bless the absent-minded and make their curse a joy to them forever!

"Abbas. Abbas el Abd, the one you rented the flat opposite to. I was just wondering if he's finished what he had in hand yet."

"Hang on a tick, sonny, and I'll go and see."

Saying this she disappears. I wait. I drum my fingers. I scratch the usual "area of low pressure" if you know what I mean and I think you do. And I wait.

Someone knocks on my door and I yell

—*God save just me and send the rest to the usual hell*—

that I'm busy. I do not wish to be disturbed. Something like that.

8

I put the receiver to my ear again waiting for the "dear old lady," who picks up after three seconds and says: "Sorry, sonny, I can hear him talking to someone. One of your friends must be with him."

When you think about things it feels, sometimes, like the things that are happening aren't really happening.

"And how are you, ma'am?"

"Crappy, son."

"Never mind. God help you."

"That's it, sonny, pray for me to the Lord!"

"O Lord!"

"That He take me."

Cough, splutter. "'Bye now!"

I swear I'll never understand the older generation.

I go and take a refreshing shower that helps me forget all the things I can't remember because I've forgotten them.

I shove on the usual dumb blue jeans with a shirt and pullover. Watch on wrist, wallet in the proper pocket. Cell phone in case on belt. Cigarettes, matches. And slam the door behind me.

I walk to the end of the street, where the minibus drivers have come up with a new unofficial stop.

"Ramses! Ramses! Ramses!"

As the tout shouts he waves at me and says: "Heh, *mizter*! Going to Ramses?"

I shake my head and make my way to the big minibus that some call 'The Phantom.'

The tout pulls me in by the shoulder like someone dragging his drawers off the line.

Then he gets off again looking for more underwear, drumming on the paneling the while to pass the time as he shouts: "This way and watch your step! (Bam bam bam!) Ramses! (Bam bam bam!) Coming with us, miss?"

In gets a petticoat.

(Bam bam bam!)

In gets an undershirt.

(Bam bam bam!)

"You, sonny?"

In gets a pair of boxers.

"All Helpful All Wise All Giving All Gener. . . ! Something wrong, *mizter*?!"

"What do you think you're doing, buddy? Whacking cockroaches with a slipper? Enough with the bang, bang, bang. Give your hand a nice dangle for a bit."

"What's it to you, buddy? Someone bang *you*?"

Have a horrible day!

"'Someone bang you?' Whoa! You want to try out your smartass cracks on me? Wise up. I've been around since before your mommy peeled your daddy's banana."

"Uh . . . what's that mean?"

That's right. Back off and try and pretend to be at least semi-human.

A giant materializes out of nowhere and gives the tout a telling off, then turns to me and says:

"Apologies. Your rights are as dear to me as the hairs on my head" (of which Mendel's laws have left precisely five).

"Aren't you ashamed, boy, talking dirty to the customers in front of me? Isn't my moustache" (which is big enough to make anyone else a goatee) "big enough to get a little respect around here??"

I settle back in the uncomfortable foam seat ignoring the curious looks of my fellow passengers and reward my lips, capable of tossing off abuse in all weathers, by lobbing a cigarette in their direction and immediately lighting its end; soon I'm comfortably dragging on its contaminated air.

I don't know how much time passes before this canful of performing animals fills up but I come to when the giant himself leaps behind the steering wheel and shoves a tape into the cassette player.

He turns the key.

"Teet ta-teet taata!"

go the horns of the cars, mimicking a well-known obscenity, as he cuts in front of them without warning to enter the stream of traffic.

A driver shouts from his window: "Hey, you! First day behind the wheel?"

The driver delivers a melodious snort of disgust and says: "Me?? I've driven further in reverse, sonny, than you've driven forwards. Go to hell and God speed!"

More teet ta-teet taata back and forth and everyone goes his own way.

The tout pokes his finger in the faces of the pedestrians and yells: "Ramseeeeeeeeeeeeees?"

I hand my fare to the person sitting next to me: "Pass it along." My face is in the open window. With my thumb and middle finger I flick what's left of my cigarette out of the window.

A passenger sitting in front of me spits out of his window and the post office rejects it as "Unknown at this Address." The gob, God bless it, re-enters the car, the air stream taking upon itself to deliver it directly to my face.

And the result?

I wipe off the adherent filth and reward my lips with a whole cartonful of cigarettes.

This time I'm careful to close the window and content myself with just looking at what's going on outside.

On my right I can see the driver of an American luxury car rubbing his hand over an unresisting white knee.

I envy the equitable way in which he apportions his finger time—a bit for the knee, then a bit for the gear stick. Knee, gear stick, knee, gear stick . . . (waiting perhaps for the gear stick to calm down).

Lords of the World, inventors of AIDS and CNN,

Lords of the World, who discovered the ozone layer and then put a hole in it—

When will the Americans come up with a knee you can caress and shift gears with at the same time?

The minibus stops at a traffic signal and a small bare-foot girl goes by.

True, her face is dirty, but it's an innocent dirt. She goes up to a red car with a well-off-looking guy at the wheel and tries to interest him in buying a packet of paper hankies, *God increase your wealth!*

He pushes her, this well-off-looking guy. He pushes the little girl with a hand sporting a gold ring on the fourth finger. He pushes her so roughly that the fragile little girl can't stand up and falls to the ground, and the packets of hankies propagate around her on the grungy pavement.

This is where the ladies of the night are born . . . in plain day-light.

Soon the little girl's body will be converted into circles that will accept the geometrical abuse of any miserable oblong.

May the hormonal conscience of our "brother Arabs" guard her well!

God bless the property rights that turn people into things that can be priced and given "use by" dates!

God bless the charity of the credit card!

We like to say that we hold our "little innocents" "dear." So **TEAR AT HER,** so long as you're gonna pay!

Let our tourist slogan in the future be Altruism, Not Egotism!

The little girl cries.

The light changes and the minibus takes off, while the voice
of Abd el Wahhab wafts from somewhere singing:

Do you know why?
Don't ask why.
Do you know why?

Under a sky polluted with hatred and smoke, what kind of
creatures are these that can breathe and multiply?

Are we seeing the survival of the most corrupt
or the corruption of the best survivors?

"Ramses and the end of the line, ladies and gentlemen."

Abbas says I'm suffering from heavy-duty depression.

To hell with good old Abbas.

Chapter 3

Don't believe her.
She will swear to you by all that is holy and will call on God
to strike her blind, if she, of all people, is a liar.
She will caress your beard, which has sprouted all on its own,
and we all know how soothing touch is to the face.
This is the truth in all its cruelty, so do as you damn well please.

FOR ALMOST TEN YEARS I WORKED IN A SARDINE CAN BEARING A
sign saying
"Amerco Video Film"
It was my pleasure to define for the exhausted and torment-
ed how to "let the world go screw itself."
Leave your nice starched life on its hanger or drop it heed-
lessly on the floor.
Chill, man.
Loosen up.
Merge with an alternative to your by now no longer existent
life and **BE** your favorite hero.

"Amerco Video Film"

Here it's not you that matters, or your color, or the size of your tragedy.

Here you won't find the answers but you can obliterate the questions.

Here

You are you.

You are the exhausted accountant who's just got home from his loathsome job—

Goddamn the balance of payments.

To hell with borrower and lender alike.

Fine. For you I have my secret exorcism. . . .

WATCH Michael Douglas in his latest movie.

"But I have to explain one thing, sir. This movie's going to make problems for you."

"Problems?"

"Like you won't be able to answer the phone and your tea'll go cold and your boss is going to make trouble for your good self because you'll definitely get in to work late tomorrow."

He smiles, swallows the bait like a white man, pays the usual gratuity, and leaves.

Enter a buxom daughter of the gentry from AUC (a.k.a. the American University in Cairo, or, according to some smartasses, "Are U a Charlatan?") to ask me about a movie that (for eminently sound reasons) hasn't been released in Egypt.

I ignore her belly button and smooth thighs, a quick glance indicating that *le boyfriend* is waiting for her outside.

"I am most awfully sorry but . . ."

She turns to go and I continue,

"I have it at home but it's not for rent."

"Really?!"

Anything but 'really'! Yes of course really! Would I mess around with you, baby?

Lots of "Please!"s and "Pretty please!"s and for almost a minute I have the sweet young thing pasted into my album of slaves, where the girls beg forever.

She'd never feed me grapes in bed in the morning, or release her moan of submission into my ear.

But it's enough:

The stuck-up fox is begging sufficiently genuinely to satisfy my well-known sadism.

God bless my favorite bar of soap!

I tell her that my hobby of sniffing bank notes re-invigorates the wisdom of my decisions and leave the matter of how much up to her, whereupon she produces from her leather purse a note of a denomination I didn't know had even been created yet.

I say the movie will be there tomorrow and off she goes to take the glad tidings to her faggoty friend.

You're the medical student with the glasses like shop windows. Medical curricula designed to treat the patients and kill the doctors—"If Montgomery's glands appear on the breasts of a statue of Venus, what are the phases of hepatitis in patients with Bollock's Disease?"

WATCH Robert De Niro in *Cape Fear* and you'll thank me later. Abbas says my childhood wasn't normal but all I say is it was different.

I was an orphan and my Uncle Awni took charge of my upbringing. That's Awni the well-known psychologist. Maybe you've heard of him.

At the beginning Awni was content to play the role of "the attentive listener"—you said everything and he said nothing. He wouldn't mess with your painful memories and he wouldn't squeeze your psychic pimples.

He wouldn't cut the throat of your childhood and unlike Freud he wouldn't strap your behavior to your anus.

Awni would never abuse your confidences and he didn't care if you tried to get out of paying tips or omitted to deploy your voice for the good of the Motherland.

But you couldn't wipe your sweat off without his permission.

"Hallo? Yes, Prof. Awni sir, it's So-and-so and. . . . Ah! . . . I'm sorry, I know it's a little late but really it's very important. . . . I've got this crazy headache. . . . Do you think I should take a Tylenol or tie something round my head?"

"Excuse me, Prof. Awni, it's Someone Else. . . . I'm just calling to ask you something. . . . You see, today's Thursday and my lady wife feels like having a good time tonight. Do you think I should do the funky monkey with the pussy or smack her with the back of my hand?"

"I'm Blah-blah and I was going to ask. . . ."

WATCH Richard Gere in *Final Analysis* and you'll thank your Uncle Awni later.

"When I'm taken short, should I do wee-wee in the street or hold it in till I get home?"

According to the Trinity of Phobias theory invented by my Uncle Awni, every one of us suffers from at least three sorts of phobia.

You are the spinster with the slight squint and the metal braces on her teeth:

Calling all fruit lovers—

Who'll buy a piece rotting unpicked on the tree?

A jack-hammer split the head of any who does not come forward this instant to ask for the hand of Miss R.O.S.E., white, of curvaceous figure and forty-three springs, who owns a furnished apartment and seeks a husband who holds matrimony in holy awe!

WATCH Meg Ryan in *When Harry Met Sally* and, uh. . . . Are you seeing anyone?

If Awni were to come back from America, he wouldn't think twice before issuing his definitive judgment.

The Trinity of Phobias in a patient of this sort would be:

Anuptaphobia—fear of not being married.

Catagelophobia—fear of being exposed to ridicule.

Macrophobia—fear of long waits.

You're the one who failed the Secondary General exam and you've got that hostile "look" and the big mouth.

Knowledge doesn't come from the mind, or the academic grind. . . . Knowledge comes from the "sack"

and flob on the one who thought up morning roll-calls!

WATCH Jackie Chan in *The Drunken Master*

because your trinity is:

Didaskaleinophobia—fear of going to school

Testophobia—fear of taking exams.

Hippopotomonstrosesquippedaliophobia—fear of long words.

Abbas says, "Destruction before construction!"

Destruction to all the jobs that didn't accept me!

to all the buses that didn't wait for me!

to all the long letters that my dead relatives didn't send me!

to the lifeboats that picked up the drowned bodies from the Titanic!

You're the computer technician with the loosened tie and a box of CDs in your hand.

Unskilled labor in the mines of Digitalia. An e-slave in Bill Gates' colony.

WATCH Sandra Bullock in *The Net*.

Then press ESC.

Chapter 4

Don't believe her.
She'll dance like a cobra and worm her way into the thickets
of your chest, then bury her fangs in you without hesitation—
some kinds of love are a poison that has no antidote.
This is the truth in all its cruelty, so do as you damn well please.

"Ramses, ladies and gents, and the end of the line."
I get out of the minibus to join forces with my fellow citizens.
A traffic cop stops me from crossing the street.
"The other way, sir!"
Shit. Shit shit shit.
"What other way??"
(He shoves me on the shoulder.)
"Like I said, mister, *the other way*—got it? How true the
proverb, 'Verily, He Who Understands is a Comfort and a Joy!'"
He Who Understands should turn you into a traffic signal at
the nearest intersection.
"Huh?"

Or make you a plastic bollard on the course for a blind man's driving test.

His colleague whispers a word of advice: "If he's giving you lip, he must know people. Let him cross or he'll get us shafted."

"Apologies, excellency. What I meant was, Hang on a sec so I can walk you over myself, in case one of them buggies knocks you off, God spare you all harm!"

"Them *buggies*?"

"He means a car, Excellency: the devil mucks with the pedals and, Splat! That's the end of you, Excellency."

"Where are you from, lad?"

"Minoufiya, Excellency."

"And your friend?"

"The same, Excellency."

"The Minoufi picks the fly off the top of the juice and says to it, 'Spit it out!'"

"You tell that one so well, Excellency, so well!"

"Another to the stomach?"

"I already know it, Excellency: 'See a snake, let it pass, see a Minoufi, whap his ass!' Hee hee! Ho ho! Gimme five, Excellency!"

His hand hangs in the air, and I leave it there.

"Hey! Taxi!"

The Minoufis have almost made me forget my first double love-date.

How could this *rendez-fou* be dumb and fun at the same time?!?

Dumb. Fun.

Abbas gets into passionate relationships over the phone and punts me over two girls because, as he puts it, he wants to get me out of my "social isolation."

I'm going to meet them now, for the first time, under his alias.

Sometimes my Oriental Conscience pricks me, but when it does Abbas forestalls me by quoting the old proverb "What does a friend owe a friend? A woman, a blind eye, and a lie." Hmmm! Persuasive guy!

"Okay. Make it the weekend."

Which is today. The appointments are at the same place, at the same time, for both young ladies together, one of them being called Hind, and the other also being called Hind.

He says the first says she has a well-rounded behind and the second says that her breast-feeding future is well assured (even without children).

The first is on the first floor, the second on the second, or is it . . . ?

One of them wants "a decent relationship" and the other wants to show you her favorite tattoo, because she "feels good about you . . . really good about you. . . ."

The first thinks stew is "ever so *naice*," the second says that she "just isn't in the mood, actually."

One of them sighs.

The other *ooh*s and *aah*s.

One of them. . . .

"Mohandisseen Bakery, cabbie."

And the other. . . .

"Jump right in, buddy."

I get in. I fasten the ruined safety belt and the driver cranks the meter.

My problem is I can't remember which one is "the first" and which "the second."

Maybe it's the Partacozine, though the leaflet said that the side effects were "minimal or non-existent." Or something like that.

Excuse me, or top up my leaky memory.

If I want to remember something exactly and I'm afraid I'll forget it, I send a message right away to my cell phone from an internet site.

Do you know the site www.cantrememberyourownname.com? (It's lousy, don't use it.)

Net messages take a bit of time. The reminder message hasn't reached me yet.

"Smoke?" A Cleopatra, Egypt's sweetheart.

"Just put one out, swear-to-God."

"Light up, buddy and give your lungs some goooood smoke."

"Thanks a million, but no."

"Don't worry, friend, I've got more."

"By the one who raised the price of gas and drove his subjects into a frenzy, I just put one. . . ."

"Okay okay, I believe you, Eggzellenzy" (he means Excellency).

"A totally *zympathigue* evening to you then, cabbie."

He lights his cigarette and smiles, revealing a set of teeth that even his own jaw would never cry for. He says something about the latest Ahli versus Zamalek match. And about the cruel fate that turns pantyhose boys into big-timers and the *ladies* (if I knew what he meant) who "won't give a real man an electric socket to fiddle with."

"On the right, friend."

Here's the fare—Gimme the fare. Bye—Bye.

For the last time I look at the phone screen, which is blank.

Net messages take some time. I say *some* time, not all this time.

The message still hasn't arrived. Counsel me, O Vizier! Which of them is which?

Chapter 5

Don't believe her.
She will molest your shattered nerves so she can practice her
sacred feminine power.
She will lick the pavement beneath your feet to make you
happy so you'll submit.
This is the truth in all its cruelty, so do as you damn well please.

HIS NAME IS ABBAS EL ABD.
Of all my acquaintances he is the only one to own a jam jar
for collecting lizards' tails, a practice he refers to as an "innocent hobby."
And that's not the weirdest thing about him.
If you go all feeble in his presence in front of someone else,
he'll take you aside and tell you, without beating about the
bush: "Put your fine feelings in your pocket and don't let anyone walk all over you."
Or
"If someone widens his eyes at you, blow dust in them."

Or

"He who wears a collar fears no beatings on the back of the neck."

Then he'll push you towards your opponent and tell him with a smile: "My friend here says you're the outcome of a contraceptive failure,"

and leave you facing the fate of a cockroach in a tap dance studio.

It's three in the morning.

The headache is close to splitting my head apart, maybe because I went onto Partacozine a few days ago.

I sit in the café to sip a cup of coffee (refuge, as you no doubt know, of the sick at heart).

The waiters are busy stacking the wooden and plastic chairs on top of one another.

None of them is paying any attention.

"Psst! Hey, you!"

The stranger with the black jacket.

"Hello, how are you, Mr. . . ?"

He said his name was

Abbas el Abd.

He extended his right hand so I took it with my left because I had something in my right. He asked me: "Sowassup? You still want to rent an apartment or is it 'Than-Q, but no than-Q'?"

"Certainly. I asked you. . . ."

"So lezz go."

"What??"

"Move your ass. Lezz go. There isn't much time."

"Give me a moment to pay the check."

"While you're paying I'll get cigarettes on the street and come back, cool?"

"Okay."

As soon as I say it, Abbas turns to the right and disappears and at the same moment one of the young waiters appears and I ask him: "How much, sonny?"

"Three pounds and twenty-five piasters."

"Have you got change for a twenty?"

His hand goes into his wad of change but he steals a funny look at me.

"What?"

He gives me the change and then sics his nosiness on me.

"Who exactly, if you don't mind my asking, were you talking to??"

The nosiness of strangers who make it their business to know your private vice and whether you're thinking of practicing it tonight.

"I was talking to whoever I was talking to and what's it to you??"

"Okay, buddy. Just don't push me."

"Push you? Why should I? You out of gas or what?"

He pushes my face back with his right hand and forms the other into a ball—the fake punch that street fight devotees know so well.

And like it's the last thing I need—the kid waiter wants to get a piece of me.

But he's picked the wrong guy.

I make a mess of his looks with my fist and give him a kick between the legs that will make him weep every time he examines himself.

Gamophobia: fear of marriage.

His two mates rush over to help him.

The first grabs a soda bottle and breaks its bottom off against the wall, yelling to his buddy as he lies wounded on the floor: "I've got it, Hibeish!"

The other unbuckles his belt and winds it round his hand to make a primitive whip. His pants sag a little, so he grabs them with his free hand, and—

"Here comes Shubra, the Baaad Part of Town!"—

he lets loose with a flood of fight insults.

Through the fog of childhood it comes back to me still.

Six years old.

The kitchen. In front of the refrigerator.

Awni wraps me in a blanket, even though it's summer, gives me a hard hug, and says: "Don't be afraid."

Then he opens the huge refrigerator, which he's emptied of everything in it. He presses the light switch so that it'll stay on after the door is closed.

"One day you'll understand."

He puts me inside . . . .

He closes the door.

I call out.

"Oooooy! Pleathe, Uncle! Uncle, pleeeeeeeathe!"

I scream.

"Aaaaaaaaaaaaaaagh!"

I beg.

"Pleathe, it'th me, Uncle!"

I kick. I call out. I cry. I scream. I implore.

But the fridge door doesn't open.

Mighty Freon, tell me . . .

How many hours was I a prisoner in there?

Four minutes and a half, but it was enough.

Claustrophobia: fear of enclosed spaces.

The two of them lunge toward me.

I fling the coffee cup into the air toward one of them so he lets go of the neck of the broken bottle and catches it by reflex. The other brings the belt down on my face but I ignore the pain and drag him by the belt with my left hand, so he raises his to get one in but his pants fall so he grabs on to them again.

Then I give him a box on the side of his face and he starts in on me. And the other joins him.

I could stop here and go on about the use of appropriate proverbs such as "Discretion is the better part of valor" and "A word to the wise" but such is not my nature.

I roll myself into a ball and shield my balls with my right hand and my face with my left arm while the feet pound my personal physical space.

I lose all sensation in my extremities,

And memory returns to the attack.

I'm on my bed and Awni ties my hands and feet using bandages, then takes a jam jar that's half filled with cockroaches and empties it over me. Next he turns off the light and goes out and I hear the door being locked with two solid clicks.

The tiny feet walk over my face. Over my neck. Over my arms. Over my legs.

The rustle of the wings.

Haphephobia: fear of being touched.

Achluophobia: fear of the dark.

I scream.

"Unnnnnnnnnncle!"

Automysophobia: fear of being dirty.

Welcome to Awni's world.

A **blow** to the head sends me to the world of the unconscious with immediate effect.

"Welcome back!"

The sunlight is burning my eyelids, so I open my eyes cautiously.

"Where am I??"

"Think of it as your own home."

Abbas?!

It was time to change my position in the bed, which I did with lots of pain and screwing up of my face.

"How come if you don't like fights you go around grabbing onto people's collars?"

As he said this he started playing with the zipper on his black leather jacket: Zizzzt. Zittttt.

"How did I get here??"

"The good Lord sent me just in time to save you from the mob. I threw you into the first taxi to come along and I brought you here."

"I don't know how to thank you, Mr. Abd."

"Say nothing. But do me a favor: no Mr's and don't come on all lah-di-dah with me 'cos it gets up my nose."

He went on: "Your servant Abbas . . . just plain Abbas, no sugar."

I rubbed the place where my headache was.

"But how could you take on all the kids in the café on your own?"

He opens his jacket zipper, then closes it again.

Zizzzt. Zitttt.

"No big deal."

"You beat them up on your own? 'No big deal'? Of course it's a big deal."

"Who said I beat them up?"

But. . . .

"What do you mean?!"

He said he wasn't a school kid or wet behind the ears.

He claimed he'd heard the sound of the brawl and intervened appropriately.

(Crash! Wallop!)

He claimed that if he'd "gotten involved" with them, he would have ended up worse than me.

"So I beat you up. I went for you like I wanted to make you into a pancake. Pow! Pow! Like I was shaking out a rug."

"Are you serious??"

"Of course I'm serious, kiddo. Like it was either that or it would've been curtains for you. I beat up on you to save you from your own dumbness. You should have seen it. The kids started pulling me back and grabbing hold of me, and there was all the usual 'That's enough, buddy!' and people kissing my head and trying to break up the fight."

I won't pretend that Heaven's Mighty Vault Had Fallen or anything as far as I was concerned (even if that was what did happen).

"And they let you drag me off with you?"

"Like I said, no big deal. I told them you were a known offender and I was going to take you straight to the police station to have you paraded round all the stations in the country to see if any of them had anything against you and asked one of them to come and be a witness with me. That's when they all starting pushing their friends forward—*Me?*—*You.*—*No, him!* The main thing is I got out of there with you."

Thanks. Abso-mucking-lutely.

To have to thank someone for treating you like a rug on a date with fate over the balcony railings!

He pats my shoulder and says: "Don't get mad. That's just the way it is. 'The taste of medicine was ever bitter.'"

Then he continues with another bout of . . .

Zizzzt. Zitttt.

His fragile logic seemed not unreasonable to me.

Hair of the dog. Isn't the antidote to poison a poison they dilute before they give it to you?

"Oh yeah, I almost forgot. . . . Here's your bag."

The black shoulder bag is in the corner. As he tells me this he holds out his hand to me: "Gimme fifty pounds."

"What for??"

"Pull yourself together, brother, and pay attention. Like I say, I delivered you from the jaws of death there in a taxi."

Take them, hell and damnation to the one who spawned you!

"Now I'm going to clue you into the program, my friend."

With friends like Abbas, who needs enemies?

He draws the drapes to stop the light from using the apartment as a throughway.

We agree to split the rent and then . . .

Zizzzt. Zittt.

"Come on, let me show you around."

Furniture battered but comfy. Kitchen a maze of unwashed dishes. Bathroom fine and dirty.

Pointing to the end of the corridor, Abbas says: "Forget about the second room. It's not in the deal."

"Why?"

"You'll find out later."

He makes us a lunch of tuna with thyme and lemon, stirring the mixture with the kitchen knife.

Grace. Just a mouthful to make do.

I'm stretching out my hand when . . .

suddenly . . .

a gecko (all perky and sweet) pops out of a crack in the wall and Abbas leaps towards it, knife in hand.

Schupppppp!

The blow cleanly severs the perky gecko's tail, removing its pride and joy.

Body and tail fall to the ground.

The tail writhes where it lies but the gecko keeps moving and disappears into the nearest crack, promising Abbas he'll put a moth in his soup the next time he falls asleep.

Abbas bends over and picks up the tail. He shies the knife, via the door, into the kitchen, where it crashes against the sink and falls to the floor. Then he goes over to a kind of bedside table and pulls out of it a jam jar half filled with . . . with. . . .

Crazy son of a bitch!

He tucks the jam jar under his arm, opens its top with his free hand, and lets the tail drop into the midst of its peers.

"What's that?!"

"What do you think it is?"

"Those are lizards' tails??"

"No, pears."

"You're being sarcastic."

"It's just another hobby, like collecting stamps."

"I'd call it a filthy habit, not a hobby."

"What, stamp collecting?!"

"No. 'Pears.'"

"So, great—look at you making jokes, just as right as rain."

I say we'll never make progress as long as there are people like him around—time-killers and lizard-tail collectors and so on and so forth—and that the gap between us and the West will continue so long as we treat History as nonchalantly as a student with no parents to make him study.

The West and the East.

There and here.

There they say, "In order to succeed you must go far," and when they give you a negative assessment, they say, "He won't go far."

But here they'll tell you, "Why go to such lengths?!"

"You, Abbas, will not go far."

At this Abbas explodes like a sewer pipe that can't hold the shit any more: "You want us to progress??

So burn the history books and forget your precious dead civilization.

Stop trying to squeeze the juice from the past.

Destroy your pharaonic history.

And when you've done, please, stop boring through new walls in the Pyramids.

What good will it do to discover their true entrance or where the *entrée* was where the Great Pharaoh used to receive his hand-outs from the Envoy of a Friendly Power before offering him the *petits fours*??

Try to do without the traffic in the dead.

We will only succeed when we turn our museums into public lavatories."

Abbas pulls out a cigarette and shoves it in his mouth.

Flame. Intake of breath.

And re—hoooooooooofff!—lease!

And . . .

Zizzzzt. Zitttttt.

He takes hold of his cigarette and waves it around—cough, hack, "sorry"—continuing:

Why should a company turn out a *cartouche* of cigarettes bearing the name "Cleopatra" and announcing, with great pride, on one side:

Warning

Smoking is Injurious to Your Health

and Causes Death?

Is **that** going to make you believe in a better tomorrow? Huh? The pharaohs used to carve the names of their kings on cartouches and now we only put them on everything."

He goes into the kitchen and comes out with a blue beer can with gold designs that looks taller than it ought.

He twists the metal tag and lets it fall inside the container.

He takes a long pull, like a man kissing a woman against her will. The golden liquid dribbles down his chin and he chases after it with a corner of his sleeve.

Can it be coincidence that *Sakkara*, the name of this intoxicating brew, also means "Drunks"?!

He twists the words of a song by a Late Giantess of Arab Music and sings: "Has love e'er seen *Sakkara* like this?"

Great quote!

He says:

"Do you know what the curse of the pharaohs is?

The curse of the pharaohs is that your great great-grandson should wake from his sleep and claim that his great-grandfather had paid off his debts and the world had to show him some respect.

You know how I hate to repeat myself, but what are we going to do now that everything's clear, as proven by the fact that:

Cleopatra Injures Your Health and Causes Death, and

Sakkara fulfills the conditions of the Prophet's saying that 'What intoxicates in large amounts is forbidden in small'?"

"Okay, look . . . ."

"Forget everything.

Remember you're on your own now.

On your own, imbecile!

Snap out of it before you wake up one day—like maybe your fortieth birthday—to discover you're as scared of death as you are of Hell, not because you're afraid of dying but because you're

'Afraid of dying when you've never lived.'

Your life really is your life, not a rehearsal or a blueprint.

'But I've got nothing to lose.'

Crap.

Tell yourself what you tell the others but don't believe it.

Egypt had its Generation of the Defeat.

We're the generation that came after it. The 'I've-got-nothing-left-to-lose generation.'

We're the autistic generation, living under the same roof with strangers who have names similar to ours.

This is my father, this is my mother, and these, by elimination, must be my brothers and sisters.

You shave your beard in the mirror, whistling, and then knock into your brother by chance on your way to your room, as though you were a guest from another country staying at the same hotel. And maybe you come home to a woman who fakes her orgasms only to say to yourself, with a wisdom born of painful experience:

'It can't get any worse than this.'

Pull-shit.

You need to UPGRADE your wisdom and UPDATE your experience:

The worst thing that can happen is to have nothing worse to fear.

Anyone who reads the history of most Third World countries will discover a painful tragedy. Many have been liberated by the Revolution from 'the foreign occupier' only to fall into the clutches of 'the national occupier.'

36

In a third of the countries of the Third World—approximately—you need to have an American passport if you want to be treated like a respectable citizen."

"Okay, so what do you want to do about it now??"

"They say, 'If you don't do something to someone, someone will do something to you.'

I say, 'If you don't do something to yourself, they'll do something to you.'

And now, please . . .

Do yourself a favor and don't waste time.

Discover the hidden enemy within you. Unleash him. Give him your weak points. Give him your blemishes and your mutilated heart.

Then kill yourself."

Chapter 6

Don't believe her.
She will bury her dagger deep in your weakness.
The handle's in her heart, so why is it you that's bleeding?
This is the truth in all its cruelty, so do as you damn well please.

Hɪɴᴅ ᴘᴜғғs ᴏᴜᴛ ᴛʜᴇ sᴍᴏᴋᴇ ғʀᴏᴍ ʜᴇʀ ᴄɪɢᴀʀᴇᴛᴛᴇ ᴀɴᴅ ɪɴғᴏʀᴍs ᴍᴇ:
"You're a bastard."
I smile and say nothing so she taps on her watch.
"Who'd keep his broad waiting for a quarter of an hour??"
I shrug and snap my fingers for the waiter.
"Waiter!"
He puts on an act:
"At your serrrrrvice!"
I throw my pack of cigarettes on the table between us and turn to her: "What will you drink?!"
"*Bibs.*"
"Turkish coffee, lots of sugar, and a Pepsi."
The waiter nods and leaves.

My "broad" smiles and says: "So. Made up your mind?"

"About what?!"

"About us."

Your girl talks about "us." Possibilities dance in the air.

"About us?!"

Your girl talks about "us." The warning light on your dash-board goes on.

"Don't keep it from me, Abbas. If you don't want to, say."

Ah so!—"Don't keep it from me, Abbas."

What's the poor girl going to do when she discovers that the Earth is round and I'm not Abbas?

"What do you think?"

"These things aren't about what you think or don't think. It's one word and one answer, Yes or no?"

I cudgel my brains and come up with: "I'm afraid of hurting you. Please, really, think hard about it because I don't want you to regret anything later."

"Think about it?! You and me have gone way beyond that!"

I fiddle with my cell phone looking for a message that hasn't arrived.

Would you like to play hide-and-go-seek?

Abbas says, when he's feeling good: "Don't fight things by resisting them because they'll strike back with a vengeance. Fight things by doing them—that way they lose their meaning.

Got a problem with smoking or eating chocolate?

Smoke till your lips turn into filters. Eat Cadbury bars till your teeth melt or the factory closes.

Do it till you lose your mind."

That's his philosophy, and he practices it to perfection.

"I agree."

"Brilliant."

"By the way, why don't you come sit on the next floor up?"

"Okay."

She picks up her bag but I press her hand and say: "Wait while I go and see if there are any free seats."

So she sits down again.

I go up to the second floor, and my heart rate goes up with me. There she is, the other "broad."

How do I know??

Even Einstein could work it out. Isn't she the only one without a boy?!

She examines me as I approach.

"Hind, right?"

"Hi!"

She holds out her hand and I take it.

"Am I very late?"

"I'd had it. I was just going."

"Oh no! How come?!"

"Haven't I been stuck here for half an hour. Isn't that enough?"

In matinee tones I reply: "You mean you've held yourself aloof from me for half an hour and now you want to leave me and go?"

She shoots me a look of gratitude, of the type that says, "At last, a beast who recognizes my worth!"

I just love that bashfulness that makes girls even funkier and daintier!

"*I forgive U,*" she says, dubbing herself in English.

Heavens be praised! Let the mothers ululate with joy in their houses!

"Thank you so much."

"Why are you standing up? Take a seat."

I pat my pockets à la "Wherever can they have got to?"

"What are you looking for?"

"Seems I forgot my cigarettes at home. Hold on a couple of seconds. I won't be long."

"Where are you going?"

"To buy a pack."

"What a pain. Let someone from here go get you some."

"Errrh. It won't work."

"*Why?*" she says, in English again.

Okay, my mendacious doppelganger, fasten your seatbelt and take over the wheel.

"'Cos I smoke them with a throw-away tip."

"So he brings you a pack of tips too."

"But. . . ."

Warning: Your speed is monitored by radar.

"No buts. . . . (She turns to a waiter). Excuse me!"

"Yes," he says approaching.

"Could you get us a pack of. . . ?

She leaves a fill-in-the-blank space at the end of the sentence and points to me.

I hand my license over to the traffic cop.

"Marlboro . . . red."

Then she goes on: "And a pack of tips too, please."

"At your service, Madam."

No. . . .

I will not submit to the tyranny of the Traffic Department!

I'm going to have to leave some rubber on the road.

I'm going to have to go off-road without a license.

"There's something I have to confess."

(Before Hind confiscates my number plates, which she's going to do any minute now.)

"What? Is there a problem?"

"I wasn't expecting to find you still waiting, so . . ."

"*So?*" (in English, likewise).

I sigh.

"So that's why I left a friend of mine waiting for me down-stairs in his car. Will you give me a minute to get rid of him?!"

"Don't keep me waiting."

"The whole thing won't take a second. (What?! I'm still here?!)"

She smiles.

"*Don't be late,*" she says.

I go downstairs at precisely the second that Bottom-Floor Hind is approaching the escalator.

"Where have you been all this time?"

I grab her arm.

"Come along. Where are you going?!"

"Just don't tell me there aren't any places upstairs!"

"Honey, there's places galore."

"I don't get it . . . . If there are places why are you dragging me downstairs??"

"My sister-in-law."

"You got brothers??"

As the proverb says, "The highway of mendacity is strewn with traffic bumps."

"I mean the wife of my friend who's just like a brother to me." And the traffic bumps of mendacity can shatter your half-shafts.

"Your friend's wife is just like a brother to you?!"

Funny bitch!

"My friend's like a brother to me and she's his wife. So she's the wife of my friend who's just like a brother to me. Are we getting anywhere?"

"Ooookaaay! So what's her story?"

"She's upstairs."

She sticks her hand on her hip and yowls like a lioness whose mate's come home late from the circus without a good excuse.

"So you meet your friend and his wife and start pissing around with them upstairs and leave me on my own down here?!"

"All right, just come along and I'll tell you all about it."

"I'm not budging from this spot till I understand what's going on."

"You get the weirdest ideas!"

"That's the way I am."

I scratch my chest with my closed fingers and say: "You're really a suspicious type."

"You make a date with me and leave my ass stranded here and then you talk to me about 'suspicious' and crap?!"

"Cut it out! People are looking at us."

One pair of eyes behind the counter, one behind the window of a pastry store.

"But you're the one who . . ."

I whisper to her between gritted teeth: "Cancer. She's got breast cancer and doesn't want anyone to see her now she's had her operation."

Interrupt any female and tell her that somewhere in the world a breast's been cut off and she'll pay you more attention than she ever did even to the promptings of her personal Satan.

Hormephobia: fear of shock.

Hominophobia: fear of men.

Dishabiliophobia: fear of undressing in front of someone.

"Feeling better now?!"

It's like someone interrupting you to tell you that So-and-so's had his testicles removed.

I drag her along by her arm and lead her toward a table.

"Abbas . . .I'm . . .I'm sorry."

"You have a good heart, honey."

With the coquetry of a female dragonfly she says: "Your coffee's come."

"I noticed."

"Why don't you drink it before it gets cold?"

"Here's a sip for you so you don't (shlurrrp) get upset."

"Why doesn't she want anyone to see her after the operation?"

"She's raving. She's on chemotherapy and she's raving."

"O-my-God-how-awful!"

The waiter comes in with the pack of cigarettes and the pack of tips and looks at me in confusion.

"That's right. Over here, please."

"Weren't you . . . here . . . I mean upstairs . . . Sir?"

I take the two packs, stretch out my right leg, and allow my hand to go deep into my pocket while he asks: "Shall I add it to the check here or the check upstairs, sir?"

"I'd like it all on one check."

"As you wish."

He turns to go.

"One moment."

He comes back and I bury five pounds in his pocket, reciting over them the prayer for the dead.

"Thank *you*, prince!"

So saying, he presses the on button on his smile and makes off with it still lit in search of the next *tibs*, while I say to Hind: "Wait for me here a second. I won't be long."

"You're going to go back and talk to them again?"

"What do you mean 'them'? She's sitting on her own and it looks as though he's not coming, so I'll just go and do the polite thing— Can I do anything for you? Would you like me to give you a ride home? Really, you don't need anything? Stuff like that."

She puts the straw to her plump lips and takes a good suck from the can of Pepsi.

"So why's he dumped her there all this time?"

I lean towards her and lower my voice like someone telling a secret: "When he found out she had the 'dread disease,' he took a second wife, see."

She strikes her chest like a woman in a soap opera.

"Oh-my-God!"

This got me drawn even further into the plot.

"She found out a couple of days ago and left him straight away and left the house and went to her mother's. They're meeting now to settle the divorce details."

"Poor darling! Like they say, Men are bastards."

I stand up: "Just a few seconds, okay? I'll just do the decent thing and come right down again."

"You're a champ—don't worry about it. Take all the time you want."

I swipe the two packs and go up to the second floor.

I pull out the chair in front of the other Hind and. . . .

"So? What's up?" I ask her, but she says nothing.

"What's the matter?"

Hind plays with the glass of lemonade in front of her.

"*Nothing*," she says, in English (but I'll subtitle from now on, so you don't get bored).

She falls silent. Then she throws out an inquiry: "What are you going to do about what we were talking about?"

"Honey, whatever the Good Lord decides is fine with me."

"What's that supposed to mean?? I want an answer I can tell them at home. Are you going to propose or not?"

Propose???

Abbas wants to make trouble for me and I don't know why. This thought distracts me and I start talking nonsense: "Don't worry about a thing."

"You want me to tell Mommy, 'Relax, don't worry about a thing. Abbas wants you to know that whatever the Good Lord decides is fine with him'?!"

"Could you calm down a little so we can talk?"

"How am I supposed to calm down when you're making my blood boil?"

Three women you can't get away from:

A woman who has **destroyed** you.

A woman who has **betrayed** you.

And a woman who **doesn't want** you.

It's not just a matter of taking revenge on Abbas.

Right now, if only for a few minutes, I can **destroy**, **abandon** and **betray**.

The three-in-one shampoo.

I take out a pink pill and swallow it, chased with a swig of water.

In the Name of God the Healer.

"What's my name?"

"Huh??"

"What? Don't you understand Arabic? Do you or don't you know what my name is?"

"You're Abbas."

I pull out my ID and hold it close to her face.

"It can't be!"

She tries to snatch the card from me, so my hand retreats. Then the card looks her straight in the eye and bends her to its will as, slowly, it returns. I hold it between us and she inspects it for half a minute. Then I say: "Can be. I'm not the one that's been talking to you."

Her eyes start reddening.

Daydreams of the infirm and the insomniacs.

A woman weeping, just because you aren't you.

"And the stories and talking all night and 'I want you' and 'I need you' and 'I've missed you.' All that was lies?!"

Another dab of stingey medicine on the knee is absolutely indicated.

"And you can keep all that talk for those that need it."

"You mean you don't love me, Abbas?"

Love?

What is love???

"Are you deaf? I'm telling you that's not my goddam name!"

"So who are you?"

Are you familiar with the term "crimes of passion"?

If the investigator finds twenty stab wounds in the corpse.

If you notice a smile on the lips of the perpetrator as he confesses to the charges without remorse.

How bitter a truth!

The dagger's blow will come from one you love, while you yourself remain powerless to take action.

"I'm the one who's supposed to pick up where the person who was talking to you left off."

"What? Just like that? People's feelings are just playthings now?"

Those who turn up their noses at our mistakes—which we didn't even commit—will find themselves carried to Paradise on the wings of their own disgust.

"Why shouldn't they be playthings? Even if the person who proposes to you without your seeing him believes that he loves you, how come you believe him??"

"My, my! So smart, and every inch a real man!"

"Thank you so much."

"And what possessed you to turn down an easy morsel like me?"

"I'm just not used to eating off someone else's plate."

"You're not just heartless, no. . . ."

Dear Cupid,

Block my coronary arteries. Put your cholesterol in my blood.

"You'll find someone like yourself soon."

Dear Cupid,

Dip the tips of your arrows in your ancient wound and shoot angina into my heart.

Away!

Be brave and write my name on the hooves of your steed
So the passers-by may read it whenever your haughty prancer stumbles.

"What exactly is going on??"

It's Hind No. 1, and she's just appeared over my shoulder.

Chapter 7

Don't believe her.
She is not what she seems.
She will catch you unawares as the flame catches the moth
by the wing.
This is the truth in all its cruelty, so do as you damn well please.

IF THIS WERE A NOVEL, IT WOULD NOW BE TIME FOR YOU TO STOP
and have a sandwich.

Unfortunately, however, it isn't.

This is not a novel.

No one likes to read about the torments of the demigods when
it is revealed to them what semidemihumans they are.

These are the works that go along with the critics to the lavatory to assist them in floating free of the burden of fat buttocks.

And here I'd like to make it plain to the buttocks of both
demigods and semidemihuman critics that what Abbas el
Abd was doing when he insinuated himself with his tricks
into the lives of others was not an end in itself and that I was

never more than a false witness who happened along at the right time to swear his tainted oath, and therefore . . .

I swear to you, gentlemen, that I will never tell the truth, the whole truth, or even part of the truth.

Take, for example, that moment at which Abbas extends his hand toward his mouth to remove bit by bit the remains of the food stuck between his teeth with the cover of a book of matches, which he then scrutinizes closely with an instinctive sigh. This is not really disgusting; if you don't believe me, observe him with me as he returns the same food to his mouth, masticates it, and entertains himself by spitting out further pearls of his misguided wisdom:

"If someone gives you a dirty look, pluck out his eyebrows"

and

"God makes the woman in need too snooty to plead"

and

"If someone twists your arm, cut it off."

These may not be your principles, but it's what Abbas does. Zizzzt. Zittttt.

"If someone comes at you with the jack handle, make merry on the back of his neck with your gear stick."

"Where do you get this stuff??"

"From the can of worms we're living in."

"Never in my life have I come across anyone with so much raw malice inside him. If you swallowed your spit you'd get stomach poisoning."

"Thank you so much."

"You know, Abbas, a while ago I read a nice story by some-one called Paulo Coelho. Do you know him?"

"Never even heard of his mother."

"This Paulo guy, my dear sir, is a well-known Brazilian author and . . ."

Abbas yawns and drums on his mouth like the Red Indians *woh-woh-woh-woh* so I summarize: "The main thing is, in a place in one of his most famous novels, he's telling about a kid who goes to get wisdom from some big-shot who's living on his own in a palace."

"Cut to the chase."

Ignoring his great performance I continue: "The sage gives him a spoon with a drop of oil in it and tells him to enter the palace right foot first and to look around and observe without spilling the drop of oil. The kid goes into the palace and comes out again with the oil in the spoon just as it was and right as rain. The sage asks him, 'What did you see inside the palace?' The kid tells him, 'Nothing. I was too afraid of spilling the drop of oil." So the sage sends him back again with the same drop of oil and tells him that this time he's to take note of the things in the palace. The second time, the kid stares and notes everything carefully and then goes back to him and the sage says, 'What did you see?' and he tells him, 'I saw a bunch of paintings and a bunch of carpets and a whole bunch of other weird stuff' and the sage points to the spoon and says to him, 'Yes. But you spilled the drop of oil, my little chickadee!'"

And the moral is?

"You have to enjoy the world without spilling the drop of oil you have inside you."

As I said this, I looked at Abbas through the grime on the mirror. How pleasant it is to give one's wisdom a workout from time to time!

(We do it all the time, to make others look less important, or more bad.)

"You think so?"

"Of course."

(Improve your intellectual image and the shortcomings of others will automatically appear.)

"What do I have to swear by to make you believe?"

"There is no God but god!"

"I never liked all those fancy stories and I really get pissed off by people who write like they're saying, 'I've been shaving for four thousand years and you're still calling toffees 'offees.'"

"Look, Abbas. Take it from your buddy here and then you can throw it out the window: there's nothing wrong with making mistakes. The only thing that's wrong is not admitting them."

Let's hear it for all those who showed us we're not all alone at the bottom of the glass; there are those who are even closer to the bottom than we are.

Let's kiss the hands of all those who gave us a chance to scream at them: "Get up and dust off your clothes!"

Blessed be the saint who gave us the chance to right ourselves every time he stumbled.

"I have a slightly different perspective."

"And what might that be?"

Abbas bares his teeth in a smile and says: "That sage guy wasn't a lousy sage or anything. He was just some piece of shit kid from the 'hood who'd taken ruphenol and was getting wasted on his own so he said, I'll get someone and mess with his head a bit. Like, 'Take this spoon, boyo, and wander around inside and don't spill any or there'll be trouble . . .'"

He said nothing for a bit and then went on:

"I bet you while the boy was holding the spoon and feeling his way with his feet the guy who'd taken the roofies was rolling on the ground laughing hard enough to bust his hernia. After a bit, he gets around to dissolving another couple of pills. . . ."

Zizzzt. Zitttt.

"So then suddenly the roofies up and tell him to work the boy so he can get the 'mood' up to 'hyper.' 'Boyo, take the spoon and go back and take a look at the pictures on the walls and the carpets on the floors the like of which never entered your house except for your mother to wash.'"

And the moral is?

Zizzzt. Zitttt.

"Ruphenol gives you the best high."

"Sure, but what are you trying to get at?"

Abbas says that—Zizzzt. Zitttt.—he's telling you that to arrive you first have to leave.

And there are seven rules for leaving, as is well-known from the beginning of time.

The first rule for leaving is . . .

Burn your old baggage.

I remembered the "psycho-drama" therapy sessions I'd been subjected to after I came back from treatment abroad.

You never know why what happened happened, but you search around for the blind hand of fate that pushed you into the darkness.

The lady psychiatrist **introduces** herself . . .

"I'm Blah-blah."

One of those resounding names that means nothing to anyone but its owners.

So much so that I wont even say it.

Nomatophobia: fear of names.

I'll just put parentheses around an empty space and leave it to you to pick a name.

Her name is (   ).

Come on, take your courage in both hands and write a name in the space provided. Don't let me down!

Write it in pencil so you can erase it and write another one at any time.

Join in my little tragedy and don't try to get out of it as though it was nothing to do with you.

As you can see, we were arranged around (   ) in a semi-circle on the open side of which there was an empty chair.

The Empty Chair technique. When you were in it they'd ask you to make up a "situation." (   ) would say the technique depended on imagination.

Imagine a transparent ball in (   )'s hands that she's going to throw to you, and the instant she does you have to pour out your innermost secrets without protest.

According to (   ), the transparent ball bestows special powers on its owner, like knowing your full name, and where you work, and why cats howl at night when pelted with slippers. If you smoke in secret, the transparent ball will sniff your hand and will first tell on you to your parents and then write a report to half the state's security apparatuses.

"The transparent ball gives me the right to rummage and scrabble about inside you."

If you stay too long in the lavatory without good reason, the transparent ball will request the VD specialist to visit you and read your palm.

Don't ask what happened to your privacy at the psychiatric clinic, because there it's just a hankie anyone can blow their nose into every time a germ wafts through the air.

"And the moment you've said what's inside you . . ."

By which she means: as soon as you've finished humiliating yourself

"you can throw the transparent ball to anyone else" (herself excepted of course) and so on and so forth till the ball comes back to her.

She alone has the right to withdraw the ball at any moment and throw it to anyone she wants.

The second rule for leaving is . . .

Leave without explanations.

(   ) **throws** the transparent ball toward me and says: "Throw caution to the wind and live your storm like a mouse in a teacup."

Imagine Awni on the Empty Chair and have a chat. Then sit on it yourself and speak as though you were he.

Now then . . .

A little push and you'll be there.

Making you feel like someone who finds their goods have already been opened before they can sell them, (   ) says: "Squeeze out your psychological pus.

Say words you don't like to hear. Let me push you gently to the edge."

Your life with others is nothing but pressures, and your pressures will never go away and never become less.

"That's why we are compelled to increase the dose a little."

Are you kidding?!

And what happens when one of them cannot tolerate the dose??

I stare at the Empty Chair.

"Rise . . . !"

That feeble something starts to stir within me.

Rise!

Rise!

Rise!

And now Awni starts to materialize more and more clearly.

That very same confident smile.

"Aw . . . Aw . . . Awni."

Bravo!

Now I'm stammering like a schoolboy with his face to the wall and his arms limp.

"A . . . A . . . A . . . ."

Now I'm stammering like a suspect being batted from side to side at the Bilbeis checkpoint.

"Awni. . . ."

The volume level in my head rises.

"Don't be afraid . . . ."

The voice that knows exactly what it wants.

My lips move.

Awni. Awni. Awni. Come on, inject my veins with the same drug. Connect the electric poles to my head. Cable me gently up. Put the tongue-guard between my teeth.

Save me from my old errors and turn the dial all the way to the right.

Release the swarm of moths from their captivity and let them dance in my head.

Electricity electricity electricity and more electricity.

After a standard jolt of electricity, what's happening to me seems to be happening in a parallel world.

I'm not afraid of you or them.

Nothing can hurt me here.

(Sputter sputter). "Tut tut, Uncle! You'll get me mad at you."

Don't let my streaming tears hurt you—I don't mean to (just as you, as you always say, don't mean to).

You may find my drooling a bit distasteful, but what can I do? I'm the one who's out of it.

Every time I picked up the electricity bill, I felt embarrassed. How many volts, I wonder, have passed through me?

Awni puts me on the dynamo to finish charging me.

And I've become fully charged.

Now it doesn't mean anything any more and my uncle isn't the way he used to be.

One of them, on my right, is crying, massaging my shoulder with her left hand: "Never mind."

What good to me, now my milk teeth have fallen out, is "Never mind"? Where am I supposed to cash that?

Another of the ladies is embracing me at an angle that allows her reticent breast to remain that way. An old man pats my head and someone else starts clapping and everyone joins him hysterically, in their circle around me.

Is this what Amr Diab feels when he gets down off the stage? Nausea?

The third rule for leaving is . . .

Place the magnet close to the compass.

"Please, everyone!"

(   ) is speaking and clapping her hands, not in admiration but to scatter the camels.

"I do wish, everyone, we could give him a chance to continue," says (   ).

Pity. I was about to give my phone number to one of the sympathetic ladies so we could work together intensively on a deeper human bonding.

The intractable equation of the sacrificial lamb and the empty lot to slaughter it in:

If you have the empty lot you don't have the lamb and if you have the lamb you don't have the empty lot. If you know what I mean (and you probably do).

"I want you to let go with me completely."

Submit to her and let her peel you like an orange.

And now . . .

She smiles and looks at me with an attentiveness whose meaning will shortly become clear to me.

59

"The transparent ball is with me, right here in my hands. Do you see it?"

The ball is in her hands. A burning silver fireball that rises into the air and sticks its tongue out at gravity.

An incandescent globe.

The transparent ball demands your unconditional surrender.

"And I'm tossing it to you NOW."

She tosses the ball toward me and battle is engaged. The force of a thousand lightning strikes versus a can of bully beef.

The fourth rule for leaving is . . .

Let the current take you.

I'm remembering now . . .

Winter in Cairo. I'm seven now and it's night.

The rope wrapped around my body gives guaranteed results.

Awni ties the end of the rope tightly to a horizontal pole that projects from the roof of our house and says:

"See . . . two turns to the right and a turn to the left makes a triple knot."

He starts maneuvering me so that, trussed, I dangle by my feet from the pole. There's also sticky tape to contain my moans so that the neighbors can sleep peacefully or, perhaps, improve their performance.

"No, no, no, no! You'll make me angry with you. Do men cry? Huh??"

"Mmmmmm . . . mmmm."

Awni . . .

You didn't have mercy on my agonized cries.

"Don't worry . . . It'll be daylight soon and I'll untie you."

Now you're leaving me swinging upside down like some fake night bird. Yes, fake:

I'm not Batman and this—what's beneath me—isn't the sky of Gotham City.

The problem wasn't the rain that started pelting cruelly down after you'd left.

The problem wasn't the law of gravity.

The problem was I'd got into the habit of going to the lavatory at night. So let me tell you about the moment when the warmth—much appreciated—permeated my underpants. Let me talk, so I can raise your spirits, which have reached rock bottom. There's a yellow liquid that flows and flows in a contrary direction the length of my undershirt till it soaks my face.

Close your eyes, drag and drop the Defilement icon into the folders of your brain.

Then expel the air from your nose in disgust.

If I were able to breathe through my mouth, the smell would go away, but the sticky tape deprives me of that option.

Who am I, at seven, to understand anything? If you were in my place, what would you choose? Would you live in the warmth of defilement, or die in the purity of the biting cold?

Inhale the urine and tell me, where do you think I'll be in ten years?!

Tears, urine, rain. I can't remember which of them does what any more.

The three combine in a weird "mixed drink" that soaks my hair and dribbles from top to bottom/bottom to top.

An eye that rains, an orifice that weeps, clouds that piss.

How often have I heard you repeat your favorite maxim, Awni: "To make lemonade, take water, lemons, and sugar."

The lightning flashes, the thunder roars and I swing, a thing inverted.

Shivers and shakes attack my body in turn, and now something strange happens.

61

My wailing dies gradually away and another sound starts to be heard.

A stifled laugh begins to rise and swell. The sort of audience-reaction laugh you hear in the background on *Friends*.

"Hahahahahahahahah. Hahahahaha—no, pleeeeeease!—ha. Hahahahahaaaaaa."

To make lemonade, take tears and piss and rain, and then tell me where Awni hid the sugar. *(Hahahahahahaaah).*

Let's be *(Wahahahahahahaaah)* practical and stick to the facts.

Urophobia: fear of urine or urination.

⌢ : fear of heights.

Bromidrosiphobia: fear of body smells.

Algophobia: fear of pain.

Ecophobia: fear of home.

And severe bronchial catarrh.

The fifth rule for leaving . . .

Lead him who takes you by the hand astray.

The smile of the psychiatrist—who said last time her name was Shahinda—widens.

Fine. I know how dumb it is to have to delete a name after you've got used to it but don't forget you did write it in pencil.

So now you know that (   ) is (Shahinda).

(   ), or Shahinda, says as she twists her hair, which is red, behind her ears,

"Today we're going to try out together a technique that's a little bit new."

"What? The Empty Pillow technique?"

Her face goes rigid in less time than it takes to say "phobia."

"Please. All of you who aren't with us, let's concentrate a bit."

She swivels her gaze with the neutrality of a security camera and says:

"Today's technique is a little bit difficult but the results are just fabulous."

After which, she takes out some pink pills and distributes them to every single one of us.

Then she goes around with paper water cups.

She presses a remote control in the direction of something and the theme music from *The Godfather* seeps into the room like sleeping gas. A music you can't refuse.

"Might I ask, doctor, what the pills are?"

This is said by a short, shy young man. Shahinda smiles and says:

"It's a new treatment, Alaa, called Partacozine."

You want to be unchained, to be free? You want to live your life to the full? This is your chance.

Partacozine, emancipator of the slaves in three-piece suits; never again will you need to untie your ties.

Partacozine will make your life more eventful and less painful.

"Let's go, everyone. In the Name of God the Healer."

Raise your hands to Heaven in supplication and let's all say together:

O God, save Partacozine from all evil and bless us in it!

Aaaaaamen.

"Did you know that Partacozine was much attacked at first?"

O God, curse the Zionists, the evildoers, and Your enemies, the enemies of Partacozine!

Aaaaaamen.

"And by the way, this medication is a joint Anglo–American–French product."

O God, set them at one another's throats!

Aaaaaamen.

"So why was it attacked??" asks the lady broadcaster on the last chair.

"They attacked it because there was some talk about it's messing up your brain chemistry and the cells never being the same again."

O God, may any who wishes evil to us or to Partacozine attend to his own affairs!

Aaaaaaaamen.

"But those are only very rare cases. Something in the region of one in a million."

She takes a Partacozine tablet between her middle finger and thumb and waves it about.

"Partacozine has no side effects. All it does is help your imagination. And I want you to know, everyone, that you're the first to use it in Egypt."

O God, grant success to all who wish well to us and to Partacozine, O Lord of the Worlds!

Aaaaaaaaaaamen.

"Partacozine starts working after five minutes."

Aaaaaaaaaaaaaaamen.

"Today, we're going to imagine that the Transparent Ball is inside a ball that's inside a ball."

I noticed Abbas—whom I didn't know I'd meet later—for the first time when I was on my own at the end of this session.

I didn't know then that he'd offer to share his place with me or that our agreement would be: "Meet me at the café on the corner tomorrow night."

I didn't ask him his name and he forgot to tell me—or deliberately avoided telling me—it.

He said nothing the whole time and the others ignored him, so I did the same.

And now . . .

She looks at me closely. She smiles.

"Here are our Transparent Balls. In my hands."

Cease, O Ever Repeated Rhythm, and catch your breath.

"Can you see them?"

The balls are in her hands. A fireball inside a fireball inside a silvery fireball that rises in the air like a shot from *The Matrix*. The balls incandesce.

The Transparent Balls ask to hurt you, unconditionally.

"And I'm tossing them to you NOW."

Shooo! Shooo! Shooo!

The sixth rule for leaving is . . .

Wave to the others.

Awni claims that there's a superego and a regular ego.

If the World forsakes you—which is more or less what it's there for—that abandonment may seem reasonable. But what happens if what forsakes you is the ego?

"Don't be scared."

You're just an "I" inside an "I."

Think of it as between parentheses, working from the inside out: (I(ins(**I**)de)I).

And Awni asserts—based on what Freud said—that you are nothing but "I inside I inside I."

Nothing but ten parentheses and a stupid sentence.

(I(ins(I(ins(**I**)de)I)ide)I).

How many times did he say it??

"Don't be scared."

At the time when my peers were running around trying to find the prizes in packets of potato chips and pinning Kick Me notices on other kids' backs, Awni was whispering in my ear: "Don't be scared."

Dozens of transparent rings formed and started circling around me, and an army of memories attacked as one.

"Don't be scared."

Dementophobia: fear of madness.

"Don't be scared."

Decidophobia: fear of making decisions.

"Don't be scared."

Epistomophobia: fear of knowledge.

"Don't be scared."

Doxophobia: fear of expressing opinions or of receiving praise.

"Don't be scared."

Hypegiaphobia: fear of responsibility.

"Don't be scared."

Mastigophobia: fear of punishment.

"Don't be scared."

What happened to me could happen to you, at any moment—

When you abandon everything you know to be true and are changed, without realizing it, into a totally different person.

Philophobia: fear of falling in love or of love itself.

"Don't be scared."

Euphobia: fear of hearing good news.

"Don't be scared."

Acousticophobia: fear of noise.

"Don't be scared."

Agraphobia: fear of sexual abuse.

"Don't be scared."

Allodoxaphobia: fear of opinions.

"Don't be scared."

Dentophobia: fear of dentists.

"Don't be scared."

Arachibutyrophobia: fear of peanut butter sticking to the roof of the mouth.

"Don't be scared."
Panophobia: fear of everything.
"Don't be scared."
Phobophobia: fear of phobias.
"Don't be scared."
Eleutherophobia: fear of freedom.
"Don't be scared."
(   ): fear of . . .
(   ): fear of . . .
(   ): fear of . . .
(   ): fear of . . .
"Don't be scared."

All I remember is that I was laughing when I came to. The same laugh you hear in the background of sitcoms. I was laughing.

And I couldn't stop my tears.

The seventh rule for leaving is . . .

Go with the coming of the moon.

"Hey, buddy. Where've you been??"

says Abbas as he goes on playing with the zip on his jacket. Zizzzt. Zittttt.

"Nowhere special. I just wandered around a bit."

"Awni, right?"

"What else is there in life??"

"Think about yourself a little, friend. Don't get narrow."

Abbas is starting to enmesh my ears in his web of sound.

It's not what I want, Abbas, I swear.

"Tell you what, though, the tough guy who used to take life deep into his lungs is coughing now."

In an attempt to change the subject, I ask him: "You've got a job, Abbas?"

"Naturally."

"Where are you working??"

"No particular place. Self-employed, selling Oriflame products."

"And what are they when they're at home?"

"Like eau de cologne and lightening cream for ugly faces plus face powder and lipstick, manicure stuff, Saturday night things—this, that, and a bit of the other."

"So, like beauty products?"

"Clever kid!"

"I wish you the best of luck, Abbas."

"Cool."

I don't know how long I stayed with Abbas, but it was long enough for his voice to change into the voice of a broadcaster on the Eustachian Channel.

Abbas decides that, for some reason, he's going to reap reward in Heaven because

"I'm really not happy with the way you look. Tell me, dude, how are things going on the women front?"

"I don't understand."

"Don't act dumb with me! I mean like what's with the women? Like are you seeing someone, going out, that kind of thing."

"Well, there's something but I'm not sure if. . . ."

Shahinda??

"You could say."

"So did you put the plug in the socket yet or. . . ."

"For God's sake, man, keep it clean!"

"Okay, man, okay. Keep your hair on. I just meant where have you got to?"

I look at the ground like it's suddenly very interesting and . . .

"Like we talk every day and we've gone out once or twice, that kind of thing. You know."

Was I lying?

Maybe.

"Aaaaah! I see, I see . . . . You've unplugged the current. Hmmm. So it's an eraser."

"What's that mean??"

"It means you're a blank slate, a nothing-doing, intacto, the pack's still got the cellophane on, the parrot hasn't shat in the cage, you haven't played mummies and daddies yet. You want more?"

"You're right, Abbas. I'm not even thinking about all that crap."

"Fine. Leave it to me and I'll fix you up."

"What are you going to do?"

"Leave it to me, man. Just park yourself out of harm's way for a while and hand me over your brain."

He pushes me out of the way, raises the receiver on the cordless phone, and dials some number. He presses the speaker button.

"Trinnn . . . trrr . . . click."

"Hallo?" (exhausted female voice).

"How are you doing, Hind?"

"Who is this?"

"I spoke to you a couple of days ago on the cell phone."

"Ouff. So who does that make you?"

"Abbas, girl. The wrong number guy."

"Oooooh! How are you? What are you up to?"

"I'm not. I'd still like to."

She falls into deep silent thought, and then says: "You'll find it a bit rich for your blood."

"You think so?"

"How many are you?"

"How many? Are you running a co-op, you frilly Frau?"

"What's with the 'frilly Frau' stuff?"

"'Frilly Frau' is a compliment. Anyway, you know what I mean."

(Sucking on her lip, *mwwmmff*): "God give me patience."

"Seems I've caught you just when you're all virgined up."

"Anyway, you're the one that doesn't know the system if you ask me."

"Me, not know the system?? I'm the one that screwed up the video!"

He moves with the receiver toward the bathroom, turns on the light, and I hear the sound of a zipper opening. Meanwhile Hind is saying: "That's better. Wise up and talk nice to me."

"I'll talk nicer when I know how much it'll cost."

From the speaker and with the bathroom door open, the sound of the jet of urine gets louder.

Hind asks: "What are you doing?"

"Just a quick shake of the snake."

A laugh bursts out so slatternly I almost have to clean out my ears to credit it.

"Cocky bastard! You've got me all hot to see you."

The sheer poetry of it!

Qays Ibn al-Mulawwah, were he living in this day and age, wouldn't need to halt by the remains of the abandoned encampment to strike a spark from the flint of poetry;

all he'd have to do would be to draw a heart with his piss in the dirt behind the tent.

"You know, Abbas, I . . ."

Hind goes on to say that her breast-feeding future is well assured (even without children).

And she wants to show you her favorite tattoo, because she "feels good about you . . . really good about you."

"You still haven't said how much."

The evasiveness returns to her voice.

"I'm telling you—too much for you."

"So. How much?"

"Ninety."

"Cash or installment plan?"

"Can't do it for less—you're 'crying on a dead man's head.'"

Abbas asks her gravely: "Could we cry on his chest"?

"Meaning how much?"

"Meaning fifty-five-ish . . . in that range . . . ?"

"You think you're renting a bike?"

Sound of the zip closing.

"Fifty for a bike?? Look, why don't you cop a fiver and I get to play with the bell?"

"Okay, if you're going to be sarc . . ."

He interrupts her, to the sound of the cistern flushing in the background: "Know something? This is how people lose customers. Anyway, and I say this with all due modesty, I'm personally what you might call one of those Animal Planet 'Mating Season Special' types."

Abbas emerges from the lavatory. He sniffs his dry hand and wipes it on his jacket, as Hind says: "I'm the one who loses customers? If that's the way it is, buddy, the whole thing's on me."

"On you!? What am I doing here? Buying half a pound of parmesan?"

"I knew you were just messing about."

"Listen, lady. The whole profession's about making people feel good. You're supposed to go along with the clients a bit, rev their rotors, diddle their dynamos. So anyway, tell me, are you a big girl yet?!"

"I was a big girl before your grandfather was old enough to pluck his armpits."

He interrupts her, waggling his finger in a rude gesture: "Look, let me explain something to you. You're not a pro."

"Meaning what?"

"Meaning talking dirty to the customers and mouthing off quips you didn't make up yourself. Okay, it's me that called but talk costs money, so let's keep it short but sweet: *Hallo. Hi. Here's the deal.* Then I say, *Is it okay?* and you say, *Why not?* Bam! Cut to the chase! Is that so difficult?"

"Listen, Abbas. Get your calculator and work it out. I come and go by taxi. So what am I left with to make me feel like I'm still human after being treated like a dog?"

He sits down on the couch next to me.

"Okay. Cut to the chase. Sixty."

She ponders the matter deeply and then she says: "Done."

"Cool."

"Don't forget to get lots of food 'cos I just love *hoat-cuisine*!"

Abbas throttles himself with his free hand, sticking his tongue out with a light rattle (indicating that he's about to gag) and then sits up straight and says: "The main thing is, where are we going to meet?"

"The Mohandiseen Bakery. You know where that is?"

"I can always ask."

"Be careful—there's two branches. We'll meet at the second branch which is the one facing you when you're coming from Agouza."

"When?"

"Any day that suits you. Just let me know ahead of time."

"Fine. Friday. Is three in the afternoon okay?"

"Three in the afternoon is just perfect. I'll be wearing a tight red dress with a white blouse and I'll be waiting for you on the lower floor carrying a plastic bag."

Tools of the trade.

"Fine, Honey."

He says nothing, then: "Okay. Anything else?"

Bye. Bye.

"Who was that??"

"Just one of those modern girls. A bit of a giggle, a few smart clothes, and a touch of how's your father."

He said he'd make me another date at the same place.

"Look, tiger. . . ."

He told me I'd meet them both now, for the first time, pretending to be him. A date at the same place. At the same time. For both girls together.

"And then you can see which one you want."

"Yes, but . . ."

"No butts. Let me tell you something. If you're going to live in the monkey house, you have to know how to make the monkey swing."

"Yes, but what's in it for you?!"

Abbas smiles and says: "What am I and what are you? You and I are one!"

Zizzzt. Zittttt.

Sometimes my Oriental Conscience pricks me but when it does Abbas forestalls me by quoting the old proverb "What does a friend owe a friend? A woman, a blind eye, and a lie." Hmmm! Persuasive guy!

"Okay. Friday then."

Abbas gets into hot relationships over the phone and punts me over two girls because, as he puts it, he wants to get me out of my "social isolation."

He says the first says she has a well-rounded behind and the second says that her breast-feeding future is well assured (even without children).

One of them's called Hind, and the other one's also called Hind. One's on the first floor; the other's on the second, or is it the . . . ?

One of them wants a "decent relationship" and the other wants to show you her favorite tattoo, because she "feels good about you . . . really good about you."
The first thinks stew is "ever so naice," the second "just isn't in the mood, actually."
One of them sighs.
The other oohs and aahs.
One of them is from . . .
"a Very Good Family."
The other assures you you can "cry on a dead man's head."
"Now listen up."
"Anything you say, Abbas."
Here I'd like to assure you, gentlemen, that what Abbas el Abd did was as inevitable as the appearance of unwanted hair. I was in the neighborhood, I had my ears perked and my eyes open, and I had my suspicions.
"I have just one request and that's all. . . ."
If this were a novel, it would now be time for you to put it down
And leave.

Chapter 8

Don't believe her.
She'll bury her talons in the flesh of your back
and make off with your exhausted mind.
This is the truth in all its cruelty, so do as you damn well please.

"What exactly is going on??"

says Hind as she appears over my shoulder, and the other Hind says: "Who's this?"

"Let me introduce you."

I indicate each to the other simultaneously, saying: "Hind."

So they both say, at the same time: "And what's your name?"

And they answer as one: "Hind."

If this were a silent cartoon, there'd be a ? over their heads in a shared "thinks" balloon.

The misunderstanding lasts for several moments and then the Hind who dubs herself in English says: "I'm Hind el Ghazali. . . . And what's your name?"

"Hind el Sabalibi."

The perfect weird name for what you get given by someone whose hobby is incapacitating lizards.

I point to el Sabalibi and address myself to the other one: "Hind's a colleague of mine at work."

Then I point my open hand towards the el Ghazali broad and direct my words in the opposite direction: "The Hind I've been telling you about," I say, appending a warning look.

Hind el Ghazali says to Hind el Sabalibi: "So what do think of what he's been telling you about me??"

"I swear, sister, men ought to be doused with dirty kerosene and set fire to, like on a holiday or whatever."

Hind el Ghazali shoots me a glance of appeal and says in a what-the-hell's-going-on kind of voice: "Absolutely. You're so right."

"Sure. I tell it the way I see it and no beating about the bush. Like the proverb says, 'Forget the toy-boy, just get the toy.'"

"You think so??"

"Sure. Everyone knows that. So anyway, what are you going to do about him?"

I interrupt.

"Okay, Hind. That's enough."

"Did I say something wrong?"

"Wait for me downstairs. This won't do," an
breasts a meaningful look till she understands yet more
"Aaaah! Sorry! I'll be waiting for you downstairs
and she turns to the other Hind and kisses hing into
Mwah!) and whispers to her commiseratingly: "Filthy bastards!"

I watch her descent. Meanwhile Hind el Ghazali is pulling her leather bag off the back of the seat.

"Where are you going?"

"I'm going where I'm going. What business is it of yours?"

I sprawl on the neighboring seat, make a gesture with my arm feigning indifference, and say: "I was wrong to think of telling you about how you could screw him then."

Just tell any female there's a weak point, a chink in the wall through which to get at the person who done her wrong, then leave her to think about it.

She comes to a standstill right where she is and says: "What are you trying to tell me?"

"Let it go. It's not important."

"Are you going to talk or shall I go?" Ah well, if you insist.

I ask her: "Where does he call you from?"

"From the street, or on his cell phone."

"So there you are. You just said it."

"I don't understand a thing."

As she says this she's sitting down.

"It's obvious my friend isn't pulling this trick just on you."

Her patience is exhausted.

"So what's all this got to do with me?"

"Show him up for what he is."

"You mean call the police??"

the police. You want people to talk about you?"

I do?"

osite."

a little more?"

malls!"

I told her to write his cell phone number on the insides of the doors of the ladies' toilets with a waterproof lipstick, then pass a Kleenex soaked in soda water over it because that way it would be impossible to wipe it off.

I told her to write it at the eye level of the person sitting on the lavatory seat.

And above it two words:

CALL ME
Why?

Because these things happen.

"And what good is that supposed to do me? That could make more people talk to him."

"Only on the surface. But the cleaners will report it to the management and the mall's management will want to get to the person who's doing it, who won't know anything about it till they haul in . . ."

Wickedness dawns on her angelic face and she goes on: ". . . the owner of the number, you son of a gun."

"Any time."

"Okay, but suppose no one does anything."

"It doesn't matter. You just write it in a second and a third mall till they find out who it is."

"And what if they talk to him and he tells them about me."

"I doubt if he'll say anything about you specifically, for two reasons: you can't be the only one or he wouldn't have dumped you without even seeing you, because if he'd even just looked into your eyes, he'd never have left you."

Her white face turns pink.

"Thank you."

I just adore that modesty that makes the grateful and even weaker!

"And secondly, I'll tell him you threw the whole thing in my lap and couldn't tell the difference."

The waiter comes, places the check folder between us, and says: "Sorry. I'm going off shift."

"No problem, prince."

Hind reaches out her hand towards her bag, so I grab it and say: "What do you think you're doing??"

"I'll pay for myself. I prefer to go Dutch."

I take out my wallet and repel her with a look. Her hand surrenders and she goes on: "I'm just not accustomed to it."

"So from now on, go Egyptian."

I place the check between me and the table so she can't see it and put the money in. The waiter approaches and picks up the folder with the money and the check, saying: "Just a second and I'll get you your change, sir."

"Keep it."

"Thank you, sir."

I nod, then turn to Hind: "You know, there's something else you can do."

"What's that?"

I stand up and she follows my lead.

"I have just one little request before I tell you."

"Whatever you say."

"My colleague Hind is stupid but her heart's in the right place. So she might talk to you a lot and then go and tell everything to Abbas so she can make sure you get your rights. So I . . ."

You don't want to go and let the cat out of the bag with an ill-considered phrase.

"She knows him?"

"Knows him? Of course she knows him. Abbas works with us."

"Don't worry. I won't tell her anything."

"In fact, I was hoping you'd wait for a good two minutes and then take off at your own pace, so we'd have left."

"Okay. No problem."

"Have you got a pen and paper?"

"What for?"

"I'll dictate you my number."

"I don't need pen and paper. I've got a good memory."

So I give her the house number and take the number of her cell phone. Then she asks me: "What's the number of your cell phone?"

"Actually, the phone I have with me belongs to a friend of mine who's living with me. He lets me use it sometimes but he made me swear I wouldn't give the number to anyone."

She nods understandingly.

She puts her bag in front of her and one hand beneath her cheek and enquires: "You were going to tell me something and then you forgot."

"Listen up."

. . . .

I go downstairs to the Sabalibi chick, who's burning with curiosity:

"So what happened?"

"I'll tell you when we're outside."

"Let's go."

She picks up her purse and a bulging plastic bag. I open the door for her and exit the coffee shop behind her, at which point an old woman emerges to claim that what she wouldn't have been about to receive was

"For the love of God, my children!"

Hind gives her the alms that Fate has decreed, and the woman, thrilled, launches into the following batty benediction: "Run along, my dear, may God never interrupt your generous flow!"

To which Hind responds, "Say what, lady. Why don't you think up some other blessing for me, 'cos that one would put a stop to my livelihood!"

"Taxi!"

Screeeeeech!

"Muqattam, driver?"

"Hop in, sir."

Hind stands rooted to the spot, puts a hand on her hip, and gives a flounce of well-practiced disdain.

"Why are you standing there??"

"Let's see the color of your money."

"Yuck! You really are turning out to be a materialistic girl."

I smile when I say this, then hand her the money and she gets in and we set off.

"The wife of your asshole friend turned out to be a really *naice* person" (given that it's becoming a real pain to keep showing her weird pronunciation, the latter will henceforth be subject to Autocorrect).

"'Your asshole friend'? Keep it clean, girl. Even *Harry* doesn't always have to be *Dirty*."

The driver lets out a short laugh but she doesn't get my language games.

"I don't get it."

Her face gives the impression that the stupidity that's protected her from understanding in the past will not desert her now.

The driver explains the point to her, so she laughs, obviously faking it. There's nothing worse than a woman trying to hide a fake laugh.

With the usual tired preambles she starts saying: "No, it's a shame. . . . Really a shame . . . but by the way . . ."

" . . . "

"Her things don't look like they've been cut off or anything."

I smile in spite of myself—women's eternal dumb jealousy of the next size up.

"Thing is, she's had spares put on."

Her face lights up and she asks: "Can you do that??"

I nod and hold my tongue for the rest of the journey. As per usual, I found the driver eyeing my 'broad' up in the mirror, so I change places with Hind, give him the look, and he beats a retreat. We arrive. I pay the driver off and he goes.

Hind tells me, as we're going up to the apartment: "There isn't a soul around here."

"So who doesn't like peace and quiet?"

I open the door and turn on the light.

"Come in, Hind . . . . There's no one else here."

She enters, leaves her things on the floor, and goes toward the light switch. She turns it on and off, and on and off, and on and off, and . . .

"What are you doing?"

Hind says she turns the light on and off seven times to make sure it's working at full capacity. Some kind of compulsive behavior?! Who cares.

. . . on and off and on and off and on and off and on.

"Have you got somewhere I can change my clothes?"

"There's the bathroom over there."

She enters the lavatory and closes the door behind her, so I change my clothes quickly.

Hind comes out after a few minutes in her official work clothes. How I love that universal feminine uniform that makes you want to say something dumb about how fabrics and morals shrink in unison!

Hind slips into the bed next to me and comes close.

"Brrrr. Hold me close, 'cos I'm very cold. Brrrrrrrrrrr."

The cold, or just part of the show? One sentence will reveal all.

"So be cold. It's your stupid father's fault for not bringing you up well enough to know to shut the door."

She averts her face.

"You're right . . ."

She kills a tear with a finger tip and goes on

". . . but my father, God rest his soul, died years ago."

I don't know what to say.

The only apology I can make in such a situation is to ignore the call of the flesh and listen.

And she spoke at length.

At times she would suppress the stabbing of her tears, at many others expose herself to the mercy of the blade.

She spoke of her mother's illness. She asserted that she didn't know why she felt that it was a mother's role to give birth, then, whenever she wasn't feeling too old or too sick, to pray for her children. Even when lighting her cigarette she said she'd picked up the habit from her godmother, Sawsan Vice-Squad. She spoke of that furtive pleasure that compels one to slap children when their parents aren't around, to spit out of the window at the passers by, to sit staring absentmindedly at the flame on the stove.

Then she'd pick an imaginary hair off her tongue—which continued to protrude, curling upwards—in an unhurried manner befitting the etiquette of her profession (the oldest).

"Anyway, so listen and tell me if you wouldn't have done the same if you'd been me."

Have you ever tried taking a cigarette from a pack in your sleeping father's pocket?

If Abbas were here, he'd tell her: "The cigarette of the dishonorable brings no pleasure, and even if it does, the cigarette of your father—God rest his soul—makes the head ache."

But he isn't here.

She spoke of how she wept in the bathtub. Of the bruises left by her bullying brother's fingers that only layers of make-up, and an unusual outing, could efface.

The usual Oriental machismo—that machismo that blazes up in a house as the light of a female fades.

In the life of the Granddaughters of the Night some pretence has to be made of running away from home. She spoke of spending the night on the roof.

When she said, "I swear to God I'm not spending another second with you in this house," the others realized that her midnight threat in her brother's absence was no bluff.

She speaks of the feel of the cold sand on the roof and the smell of the chickens in the coop and her tears:

"I wasn't crying from the pain of being beaten up, I was crying because . . . because

. . . I felt sorry for myself."

She speaks of the chivalrous offerings of the neighbors' son, who came to her from the next-door roof: the pillow (embellished with his body fluids), the grey blanket under his arm, bean sandwiches, a cup of tea, and, to finish up with, a spliff, Candor's Best Companion (and which may be of the Morning, Afternoon, or Evening varieties, as vouchsafed by experts in mood-alteration).

She speaks of the simple neighborhood kid who knew how to open her heart (and other things that the priorities of the profession—which at the beginning wasn't one—would demand of her) or, as the neighbors' son called it, in a moment of transparent arousal, how to "undo the bow"—which makes her cry (she should be laughing) every time she hears Mohammed Sobhi say in one of his old plays, that he's "crazy about bows." She doesn't say anything about "plucking roses" or "and so Shahrazad reached the morning's shore."

Hind knows nothing about chrysalises turning into butterflies but she does know how a female gets turned from a "young girl" into an "old scrubber" (to use another idiomatic term).

Now she's a "ho"—which, according to the lore of those who know the way of the world, can only ever mean one thing: available and impugned.

She curls up on herself more and more. She feels her arms with trembling hands and jumps, without warning, to the tragedy of her sister: "My sister Rihab was dancing in her wedding dress on her husband-to-be's birthday when he died in an accident as she waited for him on the wedding dais. Year after year she bathes on the eve of his birthday—which was the very same night as the wedding—spends the whole night making herself up, puts on the wedding dress that Daddy—God rest his soul—brought her from Iraq, and it's "on with the dance," in the dark, as she weeps. . . . I understood. I could feel what she was going through. So many times I told her, 'Don't dance in the dark or you'll ruin your eyesight!'"

If Abbas were here, he'd tell her: "Tell your mother to make her drink carrot juice."

But he's not here.

Hind speaks the whole time of her wish to kill herself and says we're dead bodies that don't know it yet.

"Speaking of which, you're quite a body yourself."

She laughs with the modesty of the experienced. You want to commit suicide?

Be my guest.

Women try to commit suicide more than men but only a minority of them pull it off. On the other hand, only a minority of men think about committing suicide, but when they do, they do it right away.

That's what the statistics say. Unfortunately, ten percent of those suffering from depression succeed in one of their attempts at suicide.

How awful! Only ten percent?

Why don't Israeli NGOs assume the costs of young Egyptians who want to commit suicide? Though in that case the Secret Service would be compelled to charge Hind with working for a foreign power.

If Abbas were here, he would express the hope that this would happen to her during a war, so that the execution could be at state expense.

But he's not here.

I unloose her raven hair with my hand.

"You're very tenderhearted, you know," she says, laying her head on my shoulder.

A dark and gloomy day!

When Abbas asks how the electric plug's doing, I'll inform him that the outlet has had a melt down, perhaps because I'm "very tenderhearted."

Hind sits up straight, folds her legs beneath her, and says: "Have you heard this joke? The doctor at the Health Unit was doing a study of birth control. Every time a woman comes in, he asks her, 'What do you use, old girl?' and the old girl tells him. One says the Pill, another the Loop. Anyway, one day this huge tall woman comes in. 'What do you use, lady?' he asks and she tells him, 'The trash can,' so he gets it into his thick skull that this is just the sort of thing he's been waiting for, drives out the other patients, and sits down alone with this woman. 'So tell me, what's with the trash can??' 'Nothing to it, brother. It's just that my husband's a bit short, so I get the trash can for him to stand on so he can reach, if you get my meaning.' 'And then?' says the doctor. She says, 'Then we start doing what you're supposed to and as soon as I feel he's going to do his business I kick the can out from under him.'"

I scratch my stubble and turn my back on her in what married couples know as the pull-up-the-bedspread-and-cover-yourself maneuver.

"What are you doing?"

"What do you think I'm doing? I'm going to crash for a while."

She sits up in panic:

"Why? Don't you like me?"

"On the contrary. You're incredible."

"So what's the matter?"

She kills a tear with a finger tip and goes on

" . . . but my father, God rest his soul, died years ago."

She speaks of how she wept in the bathtub and of the bruises left by her bullying brother's fingers that only layers of make-up, and an unusual outing, could efface.

The usual Oriental machismo—that machismo that blazes up in a house as the light of a female fades.

"You got your money, didn't you? So leave me in peace."

"No way, sweetheart. I could never accept money for something I hadn't done, it wouldn't be right."

Hind wants to turn her sinful daily bread into something virtuous.

Hind isn't looking, God forbid, for the wrong wrong, she's in pursuit of the right wrong.

"Don't worry about it, woman. You can keep it."

"And I don't beg, from you or anyone else."

I sit up in bed and look at my feet.

"Hind . . ."

"Yes, Abbas?"

"I know I hardly know you from Eve and I know that what I'm going to say will make you angry, but I'm going to say it all the same."

"Go ahead. I'm not holding your mouth shut."

"You know, there's something very strange. From the moment I met you, as far as I was concerned you were a THING. Even when you went through the door of the apartment you were still, to me, just a THING, a thing to be consumed and taken and thrown away . . ."

A consumer item I wanted to use till it could be used no more.

" . . . and when you told your story, I didn't want to hear, I wanted you to shut up, I was dying to block my ears from the inside. What happened to you wasn't my problem and you specifically were the last thing I was worried about. But when I listened to you, and listened to you, and listened to you . . . despite myself you ceased to be a 'thing.' You became 'somebody.'"

She's weeping.

". . . a real flesh and blood human being just like anyone else. Flesh, but not the sort that's for eating, and blood, but not the sort that's for drinking. Flesh that feels and can be felt. Blood just like the blood that flows in my own veins."

Her smooth body is shaking she's weeping so hard. And suddenly I remember that little girl. The little girl that our great thick hand had pushed with a cruelty her frail body could not withstand.

Had she fallen to the ground? Had the packets of hankies propagated around her on the grungy pavement?

This is where the ladies of the night are born. . . .

On my bed.

Now the body of the *little girl* has been converted into curves that, from the geometric point of view, will accept the abuse of my miserable oblong.

May my hormonal conscience keep her safe.

Let our tourist slogan now be: **TEAR AWAY**, so long as it's not your own flesh!

God bless the property rights that turn Hind into something that can be priced and given a "use by" date.

Hind weeps, and my ugly history weeps along with her.

What happens to make us abandon our principles and turn, without being aware of it, into a completely different person? She comes close to me, in a state of collapse. She weeps in my arms and I pat her on the head and whisper in her ear, as though I cared: "Hushshshshshshshsh. As long as you're with me nothing can hurt you. Hushshshshshshsh."

"Wha . . . wha . . . what's . . . in . . . that . . . roo . . . roo . . . roo-oo-oom?" She points to the forbidden room.

The curiosity of the female that killed the cat, and inspired Monica.

If Abbas were here, he'd say . . .

But he's not.

Chapter 9

Don't believe her.
She'll give you her beginning while seeking your end
And she'll let you violate the sun till the threads of the sunset weep.
This is the truth in all its cruelty, so do as you damn well please.

PULVERIZE THE SAWDUST AND MIX IT WITH THE TALCUM POWDER. Close the can with the powder and shake it well. Then put it back in the bathroom medicine cabinet or on the supermarket shelf and leave, and a safe journey to you.
Or . . .
Pour a small quantity of salad oil in front of the elevator or once every third step. Then post nearby the address and phone number of the bone doctor, thus laying up reward for yourself in Heaven.
Or . . .
Break matchsticks in the keyholes of absent apartment owners, in order to improve their relations with the neighbors or encourage eyebrow-tweezer sales.

Or . . .

Next time you go to buy clothes for the Feast, take a couple of shirts to try on in the room set aside for that purpose and swap the price tags out of sight of prying eyes. The rule is fixed: two of each type, two of the same size each time. Similar prices. And don't forget to thank the salesperson for taking so much trouble.

Or . . .

Glue together the books in the public libraries, according to the following recipe:

1. Be sure to choose an appropriate time, bearing in mind that the slack periods are known to be: start of the school year; the annual move from primary to intermediate to secondary to college/start up of the vocational institutes/university exams; the day immediately following a disaster.

2. Choose a provocatively large book, i.e., one of more than five hundred pages, so that your right-eous intent may be fully realized.

3. You are at liberty to choose either an author or a topic that you hate, though a compromise between the two is recommended. (Who's going to miss *Helga Knows Not Insomnia* by Van Gousta anyway?)

4. Remove the lid on the liquid gum.

5. Pour the gum into the center of the book while flipping the pages, bearing in mind that "Knowledge is Light."

6. Stick the front and back covers of the book to the first and last pages, then cross out the author's name, using an X, as a sort of souvenir.

7. Put the book back on a shelf other than its usual shelf, preferably one that is tightly packed.

The day is coming when the last barrier separating paper-backs from bags of potato chips will disappear.

In the future, they'll put out a book on the back of every bag of Chipsy chips so that people can devour the contents and then throw it away.

The day is coming when they'll put a picture on the front of every book of a man tossing it into a trash can, and write underneath it:

Help Make the World
A Cleaner Place!

And now, let me tell you of the mysterious ecstasy that will flood your body.

An ecstasy such as you have never known before.

A riotous, sweet, but dirty, ecstasy. An ecstasy with its hair in plaits that domineers and steals and stuffs the change into its pocket.

An ecstasy that moves unhurriedly through your veins.

If you ignore it, you'll confirm your stupidity and it'll despise you and put your name on the list of those forbidden to enter its paradise.

Try to see the truth and look beyond the zipper on your pants.

Nothing can match a book that's lost its readers forever.

Do not deny yourself this pleasure; do it now, not later.

Rid yourself of your precious book.

Help make the world a cleaner place and throw it into the trash.

This may not be your own way of doing things.

But it's what Abbas does in his spare time.

In his blue shirt, Abbas starts roaming the apartment, the water dripping from his hair, which he pushes forward with one hand clenched to form a claw while the palm of the other goes back to his forehead to fix the hairline at the roots.

Then he throws his body onto the sofa sending the motes of dust flying high, to wave at him from the air.

Picking up the remote control, he aims it at the television.

Click. Channel One: a woman is pulling her hair and screaming "Ah, dear God. . . . My darling, my lion, my he-camel. . . . Gone? Nooooo!"

He purses his lips with the appropriate annoyance, then . . .

Click. Channel Three: an ad for Easy Mouzou juice (which the Muslims will soon gleefully ban. The ad, not the . . .).

Abbas scratches himself and sniffs his hand. He feels ☺ because his thing doesn't smell of cloves. Then . . .

Click. Channel Eight: *Farmer's Almanac*—". . . and after sowing the land you leave it to bear fruit, and don't forget that the crop has to be . . ."

Then . . .

Click. Nile TV: the lady presenter passes on mass dedications for an Eminem song, God bless his heart.

Abbas says that if he were in a top post at the Ministry of Information, he'd force all the women presenters to stand in the windows of the television building and beat their cheeks at the same moment, thus covering the city with a cloud of powder thick enough to make planes crash into the Cairo Tower.

Click. Channel . . . : a certain High Official is saying, "I always like to use the example of the two government employees, each of whom gets 150 pounds. Now, one of them . . ."

Abbas stretches out his hand toward the family-size bag of Chipsy chips (salt flavor) and asks me to thank God that we don't live in France where there's been a tax on salt since 1780. Then . . .

Click. Channel . . . : "My darling, my he-camel. . . . Ah, dear God, noooooo!""

He asks me what's the difference between "cohesiveness" and "cohesion," then . . .

Click. Channel . . . : "In the games class the boy is ashamed to take off his shoes because his socks have holes in them . . ."

He asks me what's the difference between "play" and "interplay."

I tell him: "Give me the remote. There's an Adel Imam movie on Channel 5."

Click. In the movie someone says, "Weak is your faith, flaccid your resolve." Suddenly a cockroach of indeterminate model launches itself toward the bag of chips that is placed on the table in front of Abbas.

Abbas looks in a famished way at the bag which the cockroach has now broken into, then closes it and, shaking it violently, makes his way toward the kitchen, only to emerge a few moments later with a dingy-colored tray.

Abbas shakes the bag up and down hysterically, places the tray in the center of the table, raises the bag above his head and brings it down on the table.

Baaaaaang!!!

The Chipsies go everywhere and the cockroach reappears on its back kicking its legs in the air like someone with poor circulation. It rights itself and bolts without a backward look.

Abbasophobia: fear of Abbas.

Abbas picks up the fragments of chips and tosses them in the direction of his mouth.

In the movie: "God decides—in the beginning, and in the end."

I ask him: "Why all the pain and suffering, man? Why?"

"Why is a letter of the English alphabet."

Then he asks me: "What's the difference between the ☺ and the ☹?"

Abbas says the utilities shaft of the apartment block is the only place where a man can read the papers in the morning when his wife grudgingly shuts up so as to be able to listen to the neighbors quarreling. Episode 7009 of the sitcom "Life," starring my neighbor and his esteemed lady wife.

"Shaaaaame on you! I can't take any more!"

"Can't take any more!? What do you mean you can't take any more?? You want me to go take care of it on the street, you old besom?"

The street on the outside, the utilities shaft on the inside, and the neighbor's wife "can't take any more."

In the movie: "How *you* duwwin?"

When, I wonder, will life be more about life and less about penetration?

I snatch the paper from the top of the television. My eye passes quickly over the second page, and I say as I turn the page:

"Heavens! Did you see what happened?"

"What?"

"It says a Russian kid aged 17 hacked the Pentagon website and downloaded MP3 songs onto it."

"Big deal. Everybody gets hacked these days. Even the government gets hacked, right before our eyes."

"You're kidding. Since when?"

"Wake up and smell the coffee! Since forever. It's been going on a long time but they've swept it under the carpet and that's the last you'll hear of it."

"All right. So why don't you hack into the news bulletin."

Click. The Nine O'Clock News. A quick shot: in the market place in Jerusalem an Israeli conscript kicks an old woman in the stomach, and Jaffa oranges fall from her hands and are squashed beneath the huge boots.

Abbas says:

"You miserable son of a bitch!"

Then he turns sentimental and asks:

"Who'll eat those oranges now?"

"You mean you're worried about the oranges and not sorry for that poor old lady?"

"What I'm sorry about is that she doesn't have any options."

Having said which he asks me what's the difference between "solidity" and "stolidity."

Stop anybody and ask them about their ambitions and then leave them to talk.

You're looking for money, health, beauty, power, without grasping the reality:

We're not looking for hundreds of pounds, we're looking for what we can buy with hundreds of pounds.

And what a pound can buy is different from what a dollar can buy.

We're not looking for money as an end in itself, as we imagine. We're looking for more options.

Isn't Hell, to simplify shamelessly, being bereft of options?

Abbas claims that happiness isn't money, health, beauty, power.

Happiness is having the option. Tell me what your options are and I'll tell you who you are.

Your car's a BMW? That means you have two possibilities for pleasure:

1. You can drive it on the Ring Road. Going round in circles is heaven for the unemployed. Gyration without beginning or end. Or similarly,

2. You can drive it into a tree or a lamp post, if you want to enjoy the experience of being protected by the air bags.

Keep your options open to the end.

On the other hand, if you drive a Fiat 128, let's face it, the only possibility open to you is to be chased by police Ataris on the Ring Road till you plow into a lamp post, if you want to enjoy the experience of breathing your last amidst Cairo's magical zephyrs.

"And those asshole sons of bitches have taken away our options."

Then he claims that the options open to the Arabs are numerous and well known.

I told him: "They have a measly three options and that's it." Security in exchange for peace.

Oil in exchange for food.

And silence in exchange for aid.

And Happy Options to you too!

Abbas says: "You're forgetting the most important option of all . . ."

"Which would be what, God willing?"

"Land in exchange for blood."

Give me my despoiled land and I'll give you your forfeit blood.

"You know, Abbas, sometimes I feel you almost know what you're talking about."

"God bless your little cotton socks, my son."

Tell Abbas what your options are and he'll tell you who you are.

I look at the reflection of my face—which I no longer recognize—in the mirror.

Smile, dear likeness!

Smile, miserable copy!

You're the **Copy** and I'm the **Paste**.

What's the difference between **Shift + F10** and **Right Click**?

There's a well-kept secret in the history of psychiatric medicine.

Ask your doctor about the Dissociative Emotional Regression technique, and let him tremble.

Let him wipe away his sweat and sink further down into his luxurious chair.

Let him tell you lies.

Let him deny and curse and protest. In the depths of his soul, though, he will know that you know.

To prepare a psychiatrist to practice his profession he is subjected to repeated self-analysis because he can't treat you for something he has himself. This is the basis of psychiatric medicine.

But every rule has its exceptions.

And the exception to the rule in psychiatric medicine is known as the Dissociative Emotional Regression technique, or DER for short.

It is also known as the Forbidden Technique.

The first person to use it in Egypt was Awni.

To keep it simple, the technique consists of the psychiatrist taking your condition on himself and exposing himself to everything you are exposed to by using a combination of imagination and reality until he reaches what Awni calls "the consummation of the glove," which is like when you put on your glove and keep opening and closing your hand till the glove takes on the shape of your hand, which is the desired end for the wearing of gloves, hence its "consummation."

Normally, you are the glove and the psychiatrist is the hand that moves you like a marionette.

What happens in the Dissociative Emotional Regression technique is the exact opposite.

You play the role of the hand and your psychiatrist is the glove. When the psychiatrist reaches the "consummation of the glove," he treats you both together. You and him.

You're the **Copy** and he's the **Paste**.

You know the waxy stuff that's used to remove women's unwanted hair?

The DER technique is the depilatory that rips off that "hair that's here one minute and gone the next."

Awni practiced this forbidden technique in secret till one of his colleagues ratted on him. A little whisper here, a big one there, and Awni's name was rubbed out from the lists of the psychiatric profession with the big eraser.

But Awni didn't give up, and this is where my role in his life comes in.

He says I was a gift from Heaven sent to him on a silver chaise longue.

Awni says he did what he did for my sake. When he took me with him to America for treatment as the world's most unusual phobia case, he just meant to guarantee my future. For all he knew, if he'd left me alone I would have continued my studies and never drunk gasoline or sniffed glue.

How could he be sure that I'd make my bed and marry his best friend's daughter, to say nothing of drinking tea in the café and cursing the government's policies like any respectable citizen?

Huh?

He decided to pursue my best interests no matter what obstacles he might encounter in his path.

Awni asked me: "Are you aware of all the privileges that are granted to guinea pigs? Huh?"

When I accompanied Awni to be treated in America, there were drugs that could turn an elephant into a baby's bottle.

Dozens of new drugs. Pills in all the colors of the rainbow. Except black.

Hair of the dog. Isn't the antidote to poison a poison they dilute before they give it to you?

The pills they give you for treatment are derived from poisons and black is not included among their colors.

100

The black pill, from whose color you recoil—and only the black pill—is the one you can keep on giving without swapping the cure for stupid side effects. Amazing. The white kills and the black cures.

And he confesses: "True, I obtained a doctorate with your very own case as the subject of the dissertation.

We're doing this for the sake of All Mankind."

Then: "Come here. . . .

Wouldn't it be a pity if you lost the villa, and the car, and the bank account, and the credit cards?"

The villa whose keys had never jangled in my pocket.

The car next to which, foot on fender, in front of Ramses College for Girls, I'd never stand.

The account at the bank where I'd never ask the teller to recount me a bundle of banknotes so I could get a close look at her tanned breasts.

The credit cards whose monthly statements the postman would never leave in the one of the doorkeeper's hands that wasn't attached to his water pipe.

To have doubts you have to have distance, and I had no distance at all.

In America, Awni took his equivalency exams and then continued practicing his technique, which had the effect of magic. He rose through the ranks of his profession till the moment came when the Egyptian state decided to "bite the finger of regret" and "restore the water of his face," and, as the least possible acceptable show of recognition, appointed him head of the department from which he had graduated.

Awni's decision was swift. He went back for one week during which it just so happened that the former head of the department, who was the one who'd snitched on him, was caught with a girl student. After that, Awni excused himself from the post and went back to America, from which he has never returned.

The DER technique is forbidden for one simple reason: If the doctor fails to cure himself, he remains a prisoner of his condition for the rest of his life.

That's what happened to Spilder Willisch, doyen of American psychiatrists, faithful son of California, and the inventor of the DER technique.

The proverb says "He who puts poison in the food will taste it in the end."

And, I might also add, the victim will die too.

Chapter 10

Don't believe her.
When she surrenders to you completely
She is preparing to crush you in an instant.
This is the truth in all its cruelty, so do as you damn well please.

SHE WASN'T A CORPSE YET.

Hind doesn't like wasting time because she's never been like other girls.

Place: Geneina Mall, the Ladies' Toilet.

Hind writes the mobile phone number on the insides of the doors of the toilets with a waterproof lipstick, then passes a Kleenex soaked in soda water over it 'cos that way, cupcake, it can't be wiped off!

I told her to write it at the eye level of a person sitting on the lavatory seat.

Above it two words: **CALL ME**

  Why?

Because these things happen.
The woman goes into the toilet to relieve herself.
The woman goes into the toilet to use something that emerges, from her handbag, to protect her.
Her sin, of which she is guiltless.
A naked fragile butterfly—and
Enter the terrible number.
The number gazes at her weakness.
The number *permits itself* to intervene instantaneously.
The number asks no permission and has no supernumeraries.
This is the number…
Zero-one-zero, six, forty, ninety, thirty.

CALL ME
010 6 40 90 30

Arkadia Mall:
CALL ME
010 6 40 90 30

Ramses Hilton Mall:
CALL ME
010 6 40 90 30

The World Trade Center:
Accept no imitations.
Zero-one-zero, six, forty, ninety, thirty.

CALL ME

There's a thing I like to get up to from time to time.
As though I was living like any other lunatic.
As though I was myself, with all the little stupidities I like to commit.

And with all the stupidities that have become—by now—part of my make-up, it was obvious I'd ask her to push it.

How far?

I told her the Ministry of Tourism would be with us.

The same tools but this time she'd add knitted gloves—knitted and not leather. I asked her to cut off the end of the index finger of the right-hand glove. I told her to go to the Egyptian Museum and buy a ticket and put up with being frisked twice, then wander around for a quarter of an hour. She was to choose a deserted area, a spot with very few visitors. Then she should go into the ladies' lavatory and do the same as in the Mall, adding the international code:

CALL ME
+20 (0)10 6 40 90 30

—and pass a Kleenex soaked in soda water over it 'cos that way, **honey**, it can't be wiped off!

Then she was to put the lipstick in the right-hand glove and twist the stick well so that there'd be enough to write the number several times. Next she should put on the left-hand glove and bend her right index finger towards her palm and return to the spot she'd picked out beforehand.

What she had to do when writing was to lean her back against the appropriate wall to avoid the security cameras and take hold of the lipstick that she'd placed in the index finger with her middle finger and her thumb and continue the good work. She should write it on the statues, the movements of the guards permitting. I begged her to try to be precise; writing back to front is difficult, though her mastery of English would make her mission easier. To help to avoid mistakes, I told her to hold a piece of paper with

CALL ME
+20 (0)10 6 40 90 30

written on it. Then she should coordinate her sense of the movement of her hand behind her back with what was written on the paper in front of her. We didn't want to end up with any unclarity as to the number because of bad writing. The paper would also help her to pretend to be absorbed in reading it, which would dispel the doubtful gazes of the security guards.

Then she should go into the lavatory and flush down the paper and the broken pieces of lipstick and delete the number from the cell-phone memory because if—God forbid—she were caught, they would search for the same number on her phone to ascertain the motive for her revenge.

Don't be angry, Abbas. You attacked first.

Isn't it you that wants to burn the history books? Aren't you the one trying to destroy our precious dead civilization?

You want to destroy pharaonic history? So tell the tourist police that yourself.

For additional information, *please*

CALL ME
+20 (0)10 6 40 90 30

Didn't you say you wanted to block the hole in the wall of the Great Pyramid? Huh?

Didn't you deny there was any point in discovering its real entrance?

For additional information, *please*

CALL ME
+20 (0)10 6 40 90 30

Didn't you wax sarcastic at the expense of the *entrée* where the Great Pharaoh used to receive his hand-outs from the Envoy of a Friendly Power before offering him the *petits fours*??

106

You want to spoil the trade in the dead and turn the museums into public lavatories?? Go tell the Minister of Tourism yourself.

For additional information, *please*

CALL ME
+20 (0)10 6 40 90 30

Chapter 11

Don't believe her.
She'll call you by your name that you do not know.
And she will swear to you that you are I.
This is the truth in all its cruelty, so do as you damn well please.

THE CELL PHONE NEVER STOPPED RINGING FOR AN INSTANT.
Cautious women's voices saying my number wasn't familiar,
it had appeared on their phones, and the rules of appropriate
behavior demanded that I reveal to them my full name and
skin color. Then the caller would ask me to give myself a rank-
ing, from one to ten.

And that's not to mention the calls that come to you via an
intermediary starting with the words "*Stay on the line!*" after
which the callers say nothing and all that appears on the
screen is the word "Call," which means they're trunk calls.

"Good morning," says Hind placing the breakfast tray in front
of me, so I decide to tease her and say: "Would that be
Morning the singer you're talking about now?"

She knits her brows, then smiles as though to say, "Help me out. I've no idea what you're talking about."

I sit up in bed, stretch, and ask her: "Why did you get up so early?"

"I'm marinating the chicken you brought yesterday to grill and I've been looking everywhere for the grill but it's disappeared without trace."

"It's upstairs on the roof."

"And the charcoal too??"

"The charcoal, the gas canister, and the gasoline. Everything except the food."

The ringing of the cell phone grows louder and Hind el Ghazali's number appears, so I hand the phone to Hind saying: "It's the wife of my friend whom we met yesterday. Tell her I've got a *réunion*."

Hind takes the phone and says: "Hallo. Hallo. Don't you remember me? I'm the Hind you met yesterday. Right, absolutely, it's his phone but he's *running*. . . . No. . . . Yes. . . . He'll be . . . done in just a short while because we're going to have a barbeque on the roof. . . . Certainly. . . . By all means. . . . Certainly, I'll tell him. . . . Good bye. . . . Good bye." She puts the phone down.

On the roof?! What an idiot!

"What did she say?"

She scratches her head and tries to remember.

"At first she didn't remember me but then she remembered m . . ."

I interrupt her: "Fine, so cut to the chase."

"I told her you were running. She said, 'Are you at work?' I told her, 'No . . .'"

"What do you mean 'No'? Didn't I tell her you were a friend of mine from work when I introduced you to her yesterday, and you go and talk to her about 'roofs' and 'barbeques' and all that crap! The roof?? What are we supposed to be doing together on the roof?"

"Don't worry about it, dear. It's like I'm just visiting you. Didn't you say I was a friend from work?"

Friends from work up on the roof?!

The cell phone rings. There's an unidentified number on the screen.

I press a button and the number appears.

Cancel?

   OK.

Hind goes on: "She asked me, 'At the Muqattam apartment?' so I said yes and . . ."

"Hold it. Hold it. She asked you, 'At the Muqattam apartment?'?"

"So why should I lie to you?"

"She didn't say where she got the address from??"

"Huh? Isn't she your friend's wife?"

Curses. Observe how the fruits of untruth pluck themselves unaided. Abbas would never give her the address unless he was forced to.

"Right, she's my friend's wife but I'm alone in the house and the apartment's in a mess as you can see. I have my friend over, sure, but she's never come with him."

"Okay. He must have given her the address."

The cell phone rings. Unidentified number.

Cancel?

   OK.

I have to say something.

"My friend doesn't know how to get here on his own. He gets lost, the area being the way it is."

"So how did he visit you before?"

"Hind! What is this? An interrogation?"

"I didn't mean anything, I swear."
I slap my side with my right hand.
"Ah! I remember, I remember."
"Remember what?"

I pull out my ID and hold it close to her face.
"It can't be!"
She tries to snatch the card from me, so my hand retreats.
Then the card looks her straight in the eye and bends her to
its will as, slowly, it returns. I hold it between us and she
inspects it for half a minute.
I say:

"Got a piece of paper and a pen?"
"What for?"
"I'll dictate you my number."
"I don't need pen and paper. I've got a good memory."

"Abbas?"
"Yes."
"You were saying you remembered. What did you remember?"
The cell phone rings. **Call** appears.
Cancel?
  OK.
"No, that was something else I'd forgotten and I just then
remembered it. So, the important thing is, she told you she
was coming, then?"
"That's what she told me."
"Very well . . ."
I push her gently on the shoulder and say: "Run along and get
on with your work. And I wouldn't be at all surprised if she
didn't eat with us."

"Whatever you say, *chérie*," she says with the slatternly delicacy that seems to have become second nature with her.

"I'll go ahead up to the roof and get everything out."

"Tee-hee. Okay, but take it easy so it doesn't go off in your hand."

"If it didn't go off in yours is it going to go off in mine?"

Hind bursts out laughing, and I leave, banging the door behind me. I go out onto the roof and roll up my sleeves. I set out the plastic table and put three beach chairs round it and start getting the tea things ready.

Time passes quickly and Hind appears with skewers of ground meat and chicken and says: "Oyez! Everyone got their veils on?!"

"Over here, funny guy."

She smiles.

The cell phone rings. **Call** appears.

Cancel?

OK.

She puts a finger in her mouth and makes a show of regressing to childhood.

"Yeth, Uncle?"

I make like I'm going to hit her and she backs off towards the burning coals, laughing.

"Okay, okay, I won't do it again."

Then she starts putting the skewers out and fanning them.

The drone of a car rises from down below so I take a look. Hind el Ghazali has arrived. She parks, looks up, and notices me, so I make signs to her to come all the way up.

A few minutes pass, the click of el Ghazali's heels approaches up the stairs, and she enters through the open door.

The Sabalibi version says hello and Hind el Ghazali offers her the tips of her fingers unenthusiastically.

Stupid, smart, whatever—Hind gets the reason for el Ghazali's lack of enthusiasm straight away and she withdraws, studiously ignoring her.

"I'll go and take care of the grill so nothing gets burned. You stay here with Buttercup and I'll give you a call as soon as they're done."

"Great, Hind," I say.

Hind el Ghazali waits till she's out of the way.

"So set my mind at rest. What did you get done since yesterday??"

"You think I'm dumb?"

"My, my, my. What's this about-face? Are you still going to insist I said things I never did?"

"You don't have to say them. I saw."

"Saw what?"

"How many people dicker with their 'friend from work' over money while she stands there with one hand on her hip wiggling away and refuses to get in till you pay her? Would any respectable work mate snatch the money out of her colleague's hand? And for your information, I'm very well up on 'body language.'"

"How do you know her hand was on her hip, or . . ."

"I was sitting by the glass façade."

"Would you care to explain further?"

"Explain what? It's all as clear as daylight."

The other Hind hums a song from a well-known film by the late Souad Hosni. She turns the skewers on the coals and fans them as she sings *Life's Turned Out All Rosy*.

The ringing of the cell phone in my pocket gets louder. A strange number appears, so I don't answer.

Cancel?

"'Clear' meaning?"

"Meaning you didn't have to lie to me and tell me she was your friend from work."

114

"What difference does it make?"

"Of course it makes a difference."

"To what?"

"It makes a difference to how safe I feel letting you boss me around."

I make a gesture of annoyance: "And so?"

Her face brightens up and she smiles and says: "I put our plan into action."

"The malls?"

"Even the museum, for your information."

Fantastic.

The cell phone gives the Special Numbers ring.

"Excuse me a second, Hind. . . . (Click) Hallo. . . . Hallo. . . . Shahinda?"

"Where are you?"

"At home. Is everything all right??"

"My condolences, sweetheart."

My face goes pale.

"For who??"

"Abdullah."

"Abdullah who???"

"Your nephew Abdullah, Awni."

I say nothing.

And nothing and nothing and nothing.

Shahinda says: "I just got a fax from America with the medical report. Abdullah tricked the nurses and jumped from the fourth floor."

And she says: "Gizer Pharmaceuticals have sent you an urgent message: What have you done about the new drug??"

I stretch my hand out to my pocket and jerk out the bottle of Partacozine. My index finger and thumb turn the cap, and it opens and falls from my shaking hand.

"You're lying."

Hind is still singing *Life's Turned Out All Rosy*.

I raise the bottle to my lips and gulp down the pink pills to the last one.

Rosy, rosy, rosy, roooooosy.

"Rise . . . ."

That feeble something starts to stir within me.

Rise.

Rise.

Rise.

Now Abbas materializes more and more.

"What were you saying, precious?"

"I was saying you're a **liar!**"

Abbas leans against the parapet and says: "Don't believe that fucking bitch."

Zizzzt. Zittttt.

I thrust the phone away from my ear and point to Abbas:

"**You shut your mouth right up. . . . You know what RIGHT UP means?!**"

Hind knocks into the table and the plates fall off and she stands there in confusion.

"Who are you talking to??"

When you think about things, it feels, sometimes, like the things that are happening aren't really happening.

"Hang on a tick, sonny, and I'll go and see."

Saying this she disappears. I wait. I drum my fingers. I scratch the usual "area of low pressure" if you know what I mean and I think you do. And I wait.

Someone knocks on my door and I yell . . .

He said his name was

Abbas el Abd

He extended his right hand so I took it with my left because I had something in my right.

I didn't ask him his name. I never learned the color of his favorite drink.
He said nothing the whole time and the others ignored him, as though he was air.

"Who exactly, if you don't mind my asking, were you talking to??"

"Who said I beat up on them?!"
But. . . .
"What do you mean?!!"
"So I beat you up. I went for you like I wanted to make you into a pancake.
Pow! Pow!
"Do something quick, boy! The kid's beating up on himself!"
Like I was shaking out a carpet."
"You know, it was the kids that started pulling me back and grabbing hold of me, . . . and all that 'That's enough, buddy!' and people kissing one another's heads and trying to break up the fight."

"Where am I??"
"Think of it as your own home."

Shivers and shakes attack my body in turn, and now something strange happens.
My wailing dies gradually away and another sound starts to be heard.

A stifled laugh begins to rise and swell. The sort of audience-reaction laugh you hear in the background on Friends.
"Hahahahahahahahah. Hahahahaha—no, pleeeeeease!—ha. Hahahahahaaaaaa."

Abbas smiles and says: "What am I and what are you? You and I are one!"

Think of it as between parentheses, working from the inside out:
(I(ins(I)de)I).
Then . . .

Zizzzt. Zittttt.

What happens in the Dissociative Emotional Regression technique is the exact opposite.
You play the role of the hand and your psychiatrist is the glove. When the psychiatrist reaches the "consummation of the glove," he treats you both together.
The DER technique is forbidden for one simple reason: If the doctor fails to cure himself, he remains a prisoner of his condition for the rest of his life.

((ins(I(ins(I)de)I)ide)I).

"Hallo? Hallo?"
"I'm talking to you, woman. . . ."
Shahinda asks me, in the name of her great love, to stop.
Now Abbas's voice rises in my ear though he's not moving his lips; that same voice that has turned into that of a broadcaster on the Eustachian Channel.

Liar.

"*Me*? Lie to *you*, Awni??"

Don't believe her.

"I'm the one who had to put up with it all. I'm the one who fought the whole world so we could be together."

She will tell you of crimes I never committed and will weep in your arms in the hope that your heart will soften or relent. She will give you of herself things that will alter your being, and you know very well how much a woman who is good at giving can take.

"I swear and I swear and I swear again, that's what happened. All right. God strike me blind if I'm lying to you . . ."

She will swear to you by all that is holy and will call on God to strike her blind, if she, of all people, is a liar.

She will caress your beard, which has sprouted all on its own, and we all know how soothing touch is to the face.

"Have you forgotten all about your sweet 'Shahi'? Have you forgotten?"

She'll dance like a cobra and worm her way into the thickets of your chest, then bury her fangs in you without hesitation.

Some kinds of love are a poison that has no antidote.

"I beg you, have mercy on me, Awni. Answer me. . . ."

She'll stretch your nerves to the breaking point so she can practice her sacred feminine power.

She will lick the pavement beneath your feet to make you happy so you'll submit.

She will bury her dagger deep in your weakness.

"Your silence is killing me."

The handle's in her heart, so why is it you that's bleeding?

She'll bury her talons in the flesh of your back

and make off with your exhausted mind.

She is not what she seems.

She will catch you unawares as the fire catches the moth by the wing.

She'll give you her beginning while seeking your end,

And she'll let you violate the sun till the threads of the sunset weep.

"Alright, I'm a liar. I'm anything you say but please—I kiss your feet—don't leave me like this."

When she surrenders to you completely

she is preparing to crush you in an instant.

And she will swear to you that you are . . .

"Awni."

I . . .

A woman weeping, just because you aren't you.

"There's no one by that name here."

I say it and . . .

Cancel?

My brain feels like it's about to explode.

OK.

I look at Abbas, who's started playing with his zipper.

Zizzzt. Zittttt.

"Okay. So what do you want now??"

"They say, 'If you don't do something to someone, someone will do something to you.'

I say, 'If you don't do something to yourself, they'll do something to you.'

And now, please,

Do yourself a favor and don't waste time.

Discover the hidden enemy within you. Unleash him. Give him your weak points. Give him your blemishes and your mutilated heart.

Then kill yourself."

"Awni," says Hind el Ghazali as the other one approaches me and takes me silently in her arms. I give her a rough push and in the recoil she grabs the table and it falls over with her.

Now that Abdullah's dead there's only me: Abbas/Awni.

I go toward Abbas, who gestures with his hand toward the parapet and says: "Go ahead, prince. This way to the jump-off point." We are neither what's left of us, nor do we resemble what we are.

"The public awaits you below, whistling and whooping. Can you hear them??"

Aw-ni! Aw-ni! Aw-ni! We want Aw-ni!

Because you want your death to fill the world, because you want everyone to see your picture and your marrow to cover the pavement.

Aw-ni! Aw-ni! We want Aw-ni!

Make a space for the curious and let them see you close up. Inquiring minds, hurry up and discover the true color of brain matter and whether brain cells are really gray.

Aw-ni! Aw-ni! We want Aw-ni!

Jump in the name of the stupidities we commit and that kill us. What could be more beautiful than to be killed by hope? I get my feet up onto the wall.

The Hind who hasn't fainted screams: "Get down, you madman! How can you do that to yourself?"

Awni! Awni!

"Get down, I say."

I look at the pavement . . . . The lined-up cars give me their collective finger, flashing their lights at me, first on the right, then on the left.

We want Aw-ni!

Hind grabs hold of the bottom of my pants and holds hard onto my legs.

She weeps: "Get down, I say."

Inside of me the parentheses that Abbas put around Awni look like this: Ab(Awni)bas.

Aw-ni! Aw-ni!

Abbas moves the parentheses enclosing Awni so that he can squeeze him the way moving walls squeeze the heroes in second-rate stories.

We want Aw-ni!

Abbas presses down on Awni, down(↓)wards

[A b (A w n i) b a s]

and he presses

[A b (A w n i) b a s]

and he presses

[A b (A w n i) b a s]

and he presses

[A b (A w n i) b a s]

and he presses

[Ab(Awni)bas]

and he presses

[Ab(Awn)bas]

and he presses

[Ab(Aw)bas]

and he presses

[Ab(A)bas]

and he press . . .

[Ab( )bas]

. . .es

[Abbas]

and . . .

I jump.

A Postscript You Can neither Stop nor Get Around

He wasn't a corpse yet.

Abdullah doesn't like wasting time because he's never been like other boys.

Place: Geneina Mall, the Men's Toilet.

Abdullah writes the mobile phone number on the insides of the doors of the toilets with a waterproof Parker pen, then passes a Kleenex soaked in soda water over it 'cos that way, Neddy, it can't be wiped off!

I told him to write it at the eye level of a person sitting on the toilet seat.

Above it two words: **CALL ME**

Why?

Because these things happen.

The man goes into the toilet to relieve himself.

The man goes into the toilet to aim something that emerges from his pants.

His guilt, for the sin he did indeed commit.

A fragile naked cockroach, stompable—and

Enter the terrible number.
The number gawks at him sneakily.
The number *permits itself* to intervene instantaneously.
The number asks no permission and has no supernumeraries.
This is the number
Zero-one-zero, six, forty, ninety, thirty.
CALL ME
010 6 40 90 30

Arkadia Mall:
CALL ME
010 6 40 90 30

Ramses Hilton Mall:
CALL ME
010 6 40 90 30

City Stars Center:
Accept no imitations.
Zero-one-zero, six, forty, ninety, thirty.
CALL ME

There's a thing I like to get up to from time to time.
As though I was living like any other lunatic.
As though I was myself, with all the little stupidities I like to commit.
And with all the stupidities that have become—by now—part of my make-up, it was obvious I'd ask him to push it.
How far?
You guess.

The
النها(END)ية

Translator's Note

Being Abbas el Abd breaks new ground for Egyptian writing in more than one way. It is, in the first place, one of those works that appears somehow to encapsulate not only the private vision of an individual writer but also the mental landscape of a whole generation—that, in this case, of the Egyptians who grew up in the aftermath of their country's 1967 defeat by Israel. What the narrator calls the "I've-got-nothing-left-to-lose generation" and the "autistic generation" is indifferent to the patriotic rhetoric that fueled its predecessors' erstwhile idealism, cynical about the political process, and disturbed by the ever-expanding gap between rich and poor without having a political program with which to confront it (and without being granted the space to develop such a program). It is a generation that looks first for its icons to American popular culture and mocks both the holy cows of the official Egyptian self-image ("We will only succeed when we turn our museums into public lavatories") and the hypocrisy of "Arab brotherhood" ("May the hormonal conscience of our 'brother Arabs' guard [the virtue of Egyptian girls] well!"). It is the culture of the shopping mall, the cell phone, the SMS, and the computer, all of which it inhabits with greater realism and comfort than its parents. It is also a generation of a relaxed religiosity whose presence—albeit little noticed by the pundits—provides a counterbalance to the discredited pieties of Egypt's establishment and the aggressive rhetoric of the fundamentalists.

These rebellions and alienations do not express themselves solely at the level of ideas and attitudes but also find a wide-open area for havoc in language. Arabic has always been characterized by the presence of two parallel idioms—the classical, which dominates writing, and the colloquial, which is the Arabic speaker's mother tongue and the language of everyday intercourse. Over the past half-century, this strict division of function has, it is true, relaxed somewhat in Egypt. Thus for some time now it has been commonplace to find the dialogue in novels written in colloquial, and there is even a small but growing number of literary works written entirely in colloquial. In more real-world contexts, new technology and new market forces are also expanding the realm of colloquial, with SMS messaging, internet chat, and advertising slogans all happening increasingly in that idiom. Indeed, some now speak of a 'culture of the colloquial,' identified, needless to say, with the young.

While Ahmed Alaidy is no 'colloquial-firster,' he does revel in the deployment of modern Egyptian Arabic in all its newfound and multi-layered diversity, mixing and matching idioms as the creative urge demands, often using the contrast for comic effect. An impeccably classical sentence may, for instance, have at its syntactical center an undeniably colloquial verb, resulting in what, from a traditional perspective, is a disorienting sense of a breakdown of borders. Nor is any one character expected to live within pre-set linguistic parameters. Abbas, for example, who generally employs a laid-back colloquial with strong aromas of the street, will shift into classical high gear when sufficiently excited. Within the purely colloquial realm, the argots of different sub-cultures, from hip youth, minibus touts, and auto mechanics to taxi-drivers and drug-users, and even the phonetic affectations of a genteel prostitute and the coded abuse language of car horns, all take a bow. Some of the group-specific language used may be unfamiliar even to many Egyptians: the author tells of how a leading intellectual assumed that the minibus tout's cry "Ramses and the end of the line" should be read as "Ramses and The Other," confusing two identically written Arabic words (and demonstrating both how rarely intellectuals take public transport and how comfortable they are with post-modernist thought). Even the language of movie subtitling—a denatured classical with a bent for euphemism and bowdlerization—is deployed for ironic effect. On top of all of this there are also of course the author's own unique coinages ("do the funky monkey with the pussy," "diddle their dynamo," etc).

And it is not only about Arabic. The rapidly growing role of foreign languages, above all English, in Egyptian life has been noted by many, some of whom even claim that the latter is in the process of replacing classical Arabic as the prestige idiom without which Egypt, it seems, cannot do. The characters pepper their Arabic with terms both up-market (such as *al-boyyi frind*) and down (such as *Bibs* (Pepsi)). One of them even uses so much English that the narrator is compelled to translate for her to relieve the reader of the ennui of her compulsive self-dubbing. The rendering of many of these phrases in Latin script, along with the insertion of computer commands and smiley faces, the use of graphic symbols at the head of each chapter, the comic-style bolding of certain words, the explosive punctuation (?!, ??, ???, etc.) and the eccentric layout lend the Arabic text an idiosyncratically semiotic appearance, and this has been followed as closely as possible in the English.

This ludic and original approach to language and the page obviously poses the translator some unusual challenges (over and above, of course, the snakes-and-ladders plot with its hidden trap-doors, forbidden chambers, and insanely brilliant manipulation of the reader, all of which the translator and the reader must face on an equal footing). While translation is ultimately an intuitive process that the translator himself is perhaps least qualified to analyze, some strategies for dealing with these challenges can be identified.

The biggest single challenge to the translator of *Abbas el Abd* may be to understand its many specialized usages (the "Ramses and The Other" syndrome). Indeed, when I started to work with an Egyptian friend on problems I had identified in the first draft, I quickly realized that much of what I had thought I had understood I had not, a problem overcome by going through the text with him line by line rather than, as at first intended, crux by crux.

Another challenge that faces the translator of Arabic works that contain colloquial of any sort is how, if at all, the translator should reflect the classical/colloquial dichotomy— for which, it must be stressed (given the common but mistaken notion that Arabic colloquial is somehow akin to 'slang' in other languages), no parallel exists in English. In my opinion this can only be done by manipulation of the overall register of a passage so as to provide the reader with at least a sense of the diversity of idiom within the Arabic.

A less pervasive but perhaps even more puzzling question is what to do with words and phrases imported *en bloc* from other languages, such as *al-boyyi frind*. Strict logic would require that these be switched into Arabic equivalents and printed in Arabic letters, but that would obviously do the reader no service. A halfway house sometimes suggests itself. Thus, *al-boyyi frind* has been rendered here as *le boyfriend*, a French anglicism that shares with the Arabic some at least of the former's social overtones, and similarly *meeting* in the Arabic as *réunion*. But what to do when Abbas shouts *"Pull-shit!"* (with the careful Arabic speaker's avoidance of English 'b' lest it turn out to really be 'p,' which does not exist in Arabic)? Should we go with "*Merde!*," as though Abbas were some kind of beret-wearing, Gauloise-smoking scion of the Francophone elite? Perish the thought! Best, in this case, to let sleeping dogs lie.

Whatever the success or failure of these strategies, and of the broader range of tricks, dodges, and sleights of hand to which the translator, largely unconsciously, resorts, credit must be given to Ahmad Shawkat, who went over it with me, as described above, line by line, and above all to the author himself, who did exactly the same, again. Needless to say, shortcomings remaining in the translation despite this process are mine alone.